Vampire Nation

Here's what readers from around the country are saying about Johnathan Rand's AMERICAN CHILLERS:

"I love your books! Everyone in my school races to get them at our library. Please keep writing!"

-Jonathon M., age 13, Ohio

"I am your biggest fan ever! I'm reading MISSISSIPPI MEGALODON and it's awesome."

-Emilio S., Illinois

"I just finished KENTUCKY KOMODO DRAGONS and it was the freakiest book EVER! You came to our school, and you were funny!"

-Ryan W., age 10, Michigan

"I just read OKLAHOMA OUTBREAK. It was really great! I can't wait to read more of your books!"

-Bryce H., age 8, Wisconsin

"My mom ordered American Chillers books on-line from your website, and they were autographed by you! Thanks!"

-Kayla T., age 11, Louisiana

"I love to read your books at night, in bed, under the covers with a flashlight! Your stories really creep me out!"

-Chloe F., age 8, California

"Man, how do you come up with your crazy ideas? I've read 15 American Chillers, and I don't know which one I like best. Johnathan Rand ROCKS!"

-James Y., age 10, Nebraska

"Ever since you came to my school, everyone has been addicted to your books! My teacher is reading one to us right now, and it's great!"

-Mark F., age 11, Kentucky

"You need to put more pictures of your dogs on your website. I think they're super cute."

-Michelle H., age 12, Oregon

"I have read every one of your American Chillers and Michigan Chillers books. The best one was WICKED VELOCIRAPTORS OF WEST VIRGINIA. That book gave me nightmares!"

-Erik M., age 9, Florida

"How do you come up with so many cool ideas for your books? You write some really freaky stuff, and that's good."

-Heather G., age 8, Maryland

"I met you at your store, Chillermania, last year. Thanks for signing my books for me! It was the best part of our vacation!"

-David L., age 13, Illinois

"A couple of years ago, I was too young to read your books and they scared me. Now, I love them! I read them every day!"

-Alex P., age 8, Minnesota

"I love your books, and I love to write. My dream is to come to AUTHOR QUEST when I'm old enough. My mom says I can, if I get accepted. I hope I can be a great writer, just like you!"

-Cynthia W., age 8, South Dakota

"Everyone loved it when you came to our school and did an assembly. You were really funny, and we learned a lot about writing and reading."

-Chad R., age 10, Arizona

"You are my favorite author in the whole world! I love every single one of your books!"

-Amy P., age 9, Michigan

"I heard that you wear those weird glasses when you write your books. Is that true? If it is, keep wearing them. Your books are cool!"

-Griffin W., age 12, Maine

"HAUNTING IN NEW HAMPSHIRE is the best ghost story ever! EVER!"

-Kaylee J., age 11, Tennessee

"I don't think anyone else in the world could write as good as you! My favorite book is NEBRASKA NIGHTCRAWL-ERS. Britney is just like me."

-Taylor, M., age 10, Michigan

"I used to hate to read, and now I love it, because of your books. They're really cool! When I read, I pretend that I'm the main character, and I always get freaked out."

-Jack C., age 9, Colorado

Got something cool to say about Johnathan Rand's books? Let us know, and we might publish it right here! Send your short blurb to:

Chiller Blurbs
281 Cool Blurbs Ave.
Topinabee, MI 49791

Other books by Johnathan Rand:

Michigan Chillers:

#1: Mayhem on Mackinac Island
#2: Terror Stalks Traverse City
#3: Poltergeists of Petoskey
#4: Aliens Attack Alpena
#5: Gargoyles of Gaylord
#6: Strange Spirits of St. Ignace
#7: Kreepy Klowns of Kalamazoo
#8: Dinosaurs Destroy Detroit
#9: Sinister Spiders of Saginaw
#10: Mackinaw City Mummies
#11: Great Lakes Ghost Ship
#12: AuSable Alligators
#13: Gruesome Ghouls of Grand Rapids
#14: Bionic Bats of Bay City

American Chillers:

#1: The Michigan Mega-Monsters
#2: Ogres of Ohio
#3: Florida Fog Phantoms
#4: New York Ninjas
#5: Terrible Tractors of Texas
#6: Invisible Iguanas of Illinois
#7: Wisconsin Werewolves
#8: Minnesota Mall Mannequins
#9: Iron Insects Invade Indiana
#10: Missouri Madhouse
#11: Poisonous Pythons Paralyze Pennsylvania
#12: Dangerous Dolls of Delaware
#13: Virtual Vampires of Vermont
#14: Creepy Condors of California
#15: Nebraska Nightcrawlers
#16: Alien Androids Assault Arizona
#17: South Carolina Sea Creatures
#18: Washington Wax Museum
#19: North Dakota Night Dragons
#20: Mutant Mammoths of Montana
#21: Terrifying Toys of Tennessee
#22: Nuclear Jellyfish of New Jersey
#23: Wicked Velociraptors of West Virginia
#24: Haunting in New Hampshire
#25: Mississippi Megalodon
#26: Oklahoma Outbreak
#27: Kentucky Komodo Dragons
#28: Curse of the Connecticut Coyotes

Freddie Fernortner, Fearless First Grader:

#1: The Fantastic Flying Bicycle
#2: The Super-Scary Night Thingy
#3: A Haunting We Will Go
#4: Freddie's Dog Walking Service
#5: The Big Box Fort
#6: Mr. Chewy's Big Adventure
#7: The Magical Wading Pool
#8: Chipper's Crazy Carnival
#9: Attack of the Dust Bunnies from Outer Space!
#10: The Pond Monster

Adventure Club series:

#1: Ghost in the Graveyard
#2: Ghost in the Grand
#3: The Haunted Schoolhouse

For Teens:

PANDEMIA: A novel of the bird flu and the end of the world *(written with Christopher Knight)*

AMERICAN CHILLERS

AMERICA'S #1 SERIES FOR MAXIMUM CHILLS!

DOUBLE THRILLERS!

Vampire Nation & Attack of the Monster Venus Melon!

Johnathan Rand

An AudioCraft Publishing, Inc. book

Book storage and warehouses provided by Chillermania!©
Indian River, Michigan

Warehouse security provided by:
Lily Munster, Scooby-Boo, & Spooky Dude

American Chillers Double Thrillers:
Vampire Nation & Attack of the Monster Venus Melon!
ISBN 13-digit: 978-1-893699-26-7

Librarians/Media Specialists:
PCIP/MARC records available **free of charge** at
www.americanchillers.com

Cover illustration by Dwayne Harris
Cover layout and design by Sue Harring

Printed in USA

Dickinson Press Inc., Grand Rapids, MI USA Job # 3712100 April 2010

VAMPIRE NATION

1

Looking back at everything that happened, I should have known right away that something wasn't right. I should have known right away that friends all around me were slowly turning into vampires. Oh, I had an *idea* that they were. But the very thought just seemed so crazy, so bizarre, that I didn't believe it myself.

Until it was almost too late.

My name is Amber McMurray, and I live in Flint, Michigan, with my brother, Brent, and my parents. For the most part, I think I'm like a lot of other fifth graders. I like computer games, television, movies, and soccer. I like going to the mall and hanging out with my friends. But what I love most is reading. Not just any books, either. I like *scary* books. The scarier the better.

The only scary books I don't like are vampire stories. There was a time when I *loved* to read stories about vampires. But, after a while, it seemed like everyone was writing vampire novels. At bookstores and libraries, even our school library, that's all I found: vampire stories. All the bestsellers, all the new releases seemed to have something to do with un-dead, immortal creatures of the night.

"Doesn't anyone write about ghosts or werewolves anymore?" I asked my friend, Michelle Adams. Michelle and I are in the same grade, but we have different teachers. She lives about two blocks from my house. We were sorting through the new books at our school library, and nearly every single book was about vampires.

"I guess that's just what's popular right now," Michelle said. "Especially with that new television series. Everybody in school is watching it."

Michelle meant, of course, the latest in a string of vampire shows on television. The newest series was called *Vampire Nation*, and everyone said it was great. Being that I was tired of all the vampire stuff, I hadn't watched a single episode.

But the interesting thing about *Vampire Nation* was that the series was being filmed right here in Flint, in a huge building that used to be an automobile factory. Each week, the episodes were filmed in the warehouse and produced in the same building. Although I wasn't all that crazy about another vampire television show, I thought it was cool that they made the television series in the city where I lived. Once a week, on Wednesday evenings, people were allowed to visit the studio and watch the production from a large room above the stage. It was called 'Fan Night,' and lots of people showed up. Sometimes, the cast and crew would hang out after filming and sign autographs.

"We should do that," Michelle said as she plucked a new vampire book from the library shelf. It was called *They Feast at Night,* and the cover featured a man and a woman with pasty white skin and fangs . . . just like a million other vampire books.

"What?" I asked.

"We should go watch a taping of *Vampire Nation,*" she replied, returning the book to the shelf. "It would be cool. If we go to Fan Night, we might even get to meet some of the stars and get an autograph. We might even meet Courtney Black."

Courtney Black was the star of *Vampire Nation*. She was in her early twenties, tall, with long, jet-black hair. She was a new star; *Vampire Nation* made her famous all across the country. Or maybe it was the other way around.

"I don't think so," I said.

"Come on," Michelle urged, as she adjusted the backpack slung over her left shoulder. Her eyes lit with excitement. "It'll be so much fun, even though I don't watch the show. Besides, I'm working on a class report about how television shows are made, and it's due in a couple days. I bet I'd learn a lot just watching how they do everything. Tomorrow is Fan Night. How about it?"

"Tomorrow's my birthday," I said.

"Even better!" said Michelle. "What a great birthday gift to yourself. It's your lucky day, and you just might get an autograph from Courtney Black! Besides, the studio isn't very far, and we can ride our bikes there."

I had to admit, it *might* be kind of fun.

I gave in. "Okay," I said. "But if I get bored, I'm leaving. I don't want to be bored on my birthday."

"Cool!" Michelle said. "We'll get to see all the vampire actors in action!"

"If we want to see vampire actors," I said, "all we have to do is look around school."

It was true. Many diehard fans of *Vampire Nation* were dressing up like the characters of the show. Some wore makeup that made their skin look white. Even some of the boys.

What's more, even some of the *teachers* had gotten into the act. Mrs. French, a fourth grade teacher, dyed her hair black. She wore a long black dress, black shoes, and her face was ashen. Every week, more and more people at school were looking like characters from *Vampire Nation*. Everyone thought it was cool . . . except me. I didn't care one way or the other.

"Don't you think it's weird?" I asked Michelle as we left the library. The morning bell had rung, and it was time to go to class. Students swarmed and scurried through the hall like mad ants. Locker doors banged, shoes scuffed, and laughter echoed from the walls.

"What's weird?" she asked as Cooper Winneker walked by. Cooper was in my class. Last year, he'd been like everyone else, just a normal kid at school. This year, his skin was pasty white, and he wore dark clothing. He looked like a fifth-grade zombie.

"Everyone seems to be copying the characters of *Vampire Nation*," I said. "They're dressing up like them, and even acting like them. It's as if they're actually turning into vampires themselves."

"I've got news for you," Michelle said. She

stopped in the hall and turned toward me.

I stopped walking and looked at her. Her pupils were a deep, liquid black rimmed in milky white, and her thick, curly dark hair draped around her heart-shaped face and over her shoulders. Her mouth was closed in a tight, mischievous grin.

"What's the news?" I asked.

"You think people are turning into vampires," she said. "Well, we *are.*"

Suddenly, Michelle's lips parted, exposing two sharp fangs. I gasped in horror, but before I could do anything, she grabbed my wrist, opened her mouth wide, and sank her teeth into my arm.

2

I tried to pull away, but Michelle had grasped my wrist with both hands. She was very strong, stronger than I'd imagined. I shrieked as I felt the two tiny pricks against my skin. But, just as I was about to scream, she let go and drew back.

"Gotcha," she said, popping the fake plastic fangs out of her mouth with a laugh. She hadn't really bitten me. She was just pretending.

I couldn't help but smile and shake my head. She'd really freaked me out!

"Yeah, you got me, all right," I said. "Have you had those in your mouth all morning?"

She shook her head. "Nope," she said. "I just popped them in a few seconds ago, when you weren't looking."

Michelle dropped the plastic fangs into her backpack and pulled out a small, round mirror, inspecting her face. "See?" she said. "This proves it."

"Proves what?" I asked.

She turned the mirror just enough for me to see her reflection in it. "Vampires don't have reflections," she said. "They don't show up in mirrors."

"That's because there's no such thing as vampires," I said, glancing at the clock on the wall. "Hey, we've got to get to class. See you later."

"I'll see you at lunch," Michelle said, and she dropped her mirror into her backpack, turned, and walked off.

Vampires, I thought, shaking my head. *Everyone's pretending to be a vampire these days. Even my best friend.*

And in class? You guessed it: more vampires. Cooper Winneker looked like one, of course, and RayAnne Schneider was now dressing like a vampire, too, and she was sitting at her desk, engrossed in a vampire book. As I looked around the classroom, I saw even more vampire books: *Dracula, Return of Dracula, Son of Dracula, Dracula's Pet Hamster, The Transylvania Connection, Night Creatures.* It seemed like everyone was reading a vampire novel. Even our teacher, Mrs. Alma, was reading a vampire book called *Daylight.* The book was hugely popular, and there was an entire series—including movies—based on it.

Mrs. Alma entered the classroom and sat. She looked normal, just like usual.

At least she isn't dressing and acting like a vampire yet, I thought.

Soon, though, I'd forgotten all about vampires and *Vampire Nation*. We had a history test that day—a long one—and it took all of my concentration. Before

I knew it, over an hour had gone by.

After we finished the test, it was time to go to the library. My classmates huddled around the desk displaying the latest vampire books. The new volumes were gobbled up and checked out within minutes.

I strode to a series of shelves to find a book to check out. The day before, I finished reading a book about giant spiders in Saginaw. I even met the author at a book signing and got his autograph. He seemed nice, but he wore freaky glasses and looked strange. I wondered if he wore those glasses when he wrote his creepy stories.

I walked past the shelves, reading the titles on the spines. If I saw one that looked interesting, I pulled it from the shelf to find out more about it.

But the strange thing was this: I kept finding vampire books where they shouldn't be. I found vampire books in the non-fiction section, vampire books in the science section. There were even vampire books for little kids in the picture book section! Crazy.

Just a good, old-fashioned ghost story, I thought. *That's all I want. A book about a haunted house or a haunted hotel, or something spooky like that.*

I searched and searched. No luck. It was as if all of the haunted house and ghost books had been replaced by vampire books.

"Miss McMurray?"

I turned. Mrs. Alma was standing at the door of the library as the last of my class filed past.

"I haven't found a book yet," I replied.

"Take just another minute or two," she said, "and come back to class."

I continued searching for anything scary—as long as it didn't have anything to do with vampires. But it was impossible. I began to count the vampire books on the shelves. In less than a minute, I'd counted almost fifty!

Then: jackpot. I found a thick, old, brown book. The spine read *The Haunting of Barker's Mansion.*

Finally, I thought. I reached out to pull the book from the shelf. The moment I touched it, however, the lights went out . . . and I was swallowed in darkness.

3

I was swimming in ink.

The sudden power failure caught me completely off guard, and I couldn't see anything. The darkness was thick and impenetrable. There are no windows in our library, so no light shined in. The only thing I could see was the glowing, red *EXIT* sign above the door at the front of the library. Carrying the book I'd picked out, I cautiously made my way through the gloom, bumping into unseen tables and chairs.

A flashlight in the librarian's office clicked on.

"Mrs. Chesapeake?" I called out.

The light swept toward me and struck me in the face. The bright beam stung my eyes, and I squinted and held the book up as a shield.

"Sorry," she said, lowering the beam. "Is that you, Amber?"

"Yeah," I said. "What happened?"

"Power failure," she said. "Odd. We're not having any bad weather. I wonder what caused it?"

"I don't know," I replied. "But I have a book to check out."

"Bring it back later," Mrs. Chesapeake said, "after the power comes back on. I can't process it without my computer. Here, I'll show you the way out."

She walked toward me, sweeping the beam of light on the floor. The frosty shaft splashed and leapt across desks and chairs as I followed her to the library door and stepped into the hall. Here, daylight came in through the windows. Beyond, the sky was gray, and the hallway was dull and leaden without the full bloom of the white florescent lights.

I walked down the empty, dim hallway, heading toward class. I could hear students chattering in rooms as I walked past, and a few of them popped their heads out the door, wondering what might have caused the power failure.

As it turned out, a couple of blocks away, a car had swerved to miss a dog. The vehicle bounced over a curb and struck a power pole that had fallen over, causing the transformer to explode and cutting the electricity for miles around. Thankfully, both the dog and the driver of the car weren't injured. The power wasn't supposed to come back on until later that evening, so we were dismissed from school and went home early.

That evening, at eight o'clock, I was on my bed, reading *The Haunting of Barker's Mansion*. The power had just come back on. I heard the front door bang open, then close. The television set blipped on, and the familiar, haunting theme music for *Vampire Nation* began. My brother, Brent, had been out somewhere, and he'd come back just in time for the show. He watched the show every once in a while, but he wasn't a huge fan like some of my other friends. My brother is more of a computer geek than anything. He's a year younger than me, but when it comes to computers, he's way ahead. He takes them apart, fixes them, and puts them back together. Brent can do just about anything with a computer. That's what he wants to be when he grows up: a computer technician or a programmer.

I continued reading *The Haunting of Barker's Mansion*. The book was about a girl my age who had been haunting an old, stone mansion for over one hundred years, and parts of the story really creeped me out. I really liked it.

After plowing through nearly one hundred pages, I got tired. I put my book on my dresser, changed into my nightgown, and climbed into bed. It was just past nine-thirty; I think I was asleep in less than a minute.

Sometime during the night, I was awakened by a noise.

A faint scraping sound. Something scratching at my bedroom window.

An old oak tree grows near the house. When the wind blows, one of the branches sometimes fingers the glass. Last spring Dad told me he was going to trim the tree, but he hadn't gotten around to it.

That's what I thought the sound was: a branch, swished about by the wind, beckoning at my window like a thin, bony arm.

I was wrong. Beyond my window, the bare tree branches were dark and still, silhouetted against the streetlight. There were no limbs scratching the glass.

But then I saw something else—a shape—and it caused me to sit up in bed, clutching the sheet and blanket. I was suddenly terrified, too afraid to move, too scared to even scream.

Outside, on the other side of the window, the face of a girl was staring back at me!

4

I tried to yell, tried to call out to Mom and Dad, but I had no voice. My vocal chords tightened like cables, paralyzed by fear. My stomach knotted, and I couldn't breathe. It felt like there was a flat, heavy weight pressing against my chest, crushing my lungs.

There was a time, years ago, when I'd had a similar experience. I'd awakened during the night, because I heard a sound outside my bedroom window. I didn't see anything, but I continued to hear the noise and didn't know what it was. I was little at the time—three or four years old—but I wasn't frightened. Curious, I slipped out of bed and looked out the window, only to see the murky face of a girl staring back at me. That's when I got scared and started screaming my head off. Mom and Dad came running into my bedroom and turned on the light. Well, there was a face in the window, all right. *My* face! It had only been my reflection in the glass!

That was a long time ago. What I was seeing now, in the softened gleam of the streetlight, was very different. As I looked closer, I could see that the facial features of the girl were not my own. It was a thin face with high cheekbones and short hair. Her chin was more prominent than mine. In fact, the more I looked, the more the face seemed familiar.

The girl came closer to the window, and I suddenly realized who it was: Brittany Collins, a girl from my class! Brittany was another girl caught up in the whole vampire craze brought on by *Vampire Nation*. She was wearing a dark sweatshirt, and her face was colorless.

What is she doing out in the middle of the night? I wondered.

Brittany raised her fist and rapped the glass with a single knuckle. The noise made me recoil, but I drew closer and slid the window open about an inch.

"Brittany?" I whispered. *"What are you doing out this late at night?"*

"I've got something really important to tell you," she replied.

"What?" I asked, wondering what was so important that she had to tell me in the middle of the night.

"Let me in, and I'll tell you," she said.

I looked at the clock on my dresser, at the glowing, greenish-blue numbers.

12:26.

"It's after midnight," I whispered. *"What's so important?"*

"Let me in, and I'll tell you," she repeated. *"It'll only take a minute."*

"I can't," I said quietly. *"Mom and Dad would freak out."*

"They'll never know," Brittany replied. *"Just let me in. It's really important."*

Two things came to mind. Number one, Brittany was asking me to do something I *knew* I wasn't supposed to do: disobey my parents. Oh, Mom and Dad have never come out and told me not to let my friends climb through my bedroom window in the middle of the night, but I was old enough to know they wouldn't like it, and I'd get in trouble if they found out.

But the second thing that came to mind: the only way a vampire can enter your house is if you invite them in. At least, that's what I'd read anyway.

Could it be that Brittany was a vampire? Is that why she wants me to invite her inside?

"Let me in," Brittany insisted. *"It's really, really important."*

For Pete's sake, I thought. *There is no such thing as vampires. Maybe Brittany is in trouble. Maybe she needs my help. If so, Mom and Dad would understand. They would be glad I was helping a friend.*

I reached up and was about to open the window

and allow her to climb in, but a reflection in the glass caught my attention. It was the dark, hazy reflection of the large, rectangular mirror behind me, on my dresser. In the window, I could see the reflection of the back of my head and my shoulders in the mirror. I could see the reflection of the dark, leafless oak tree, and the haunting glow of streetlights. In the mirror, I saw a couple of parked cars on the street . . . but that was all. I remembered what Michelle had told me, about how you can't see the reflection of a vampire in a mirror.

There was no reflection of Brittany in the mirror on my dresser!

5

Cold blades of fear knifed deep into my chest. My legs trembled, and I thought my knees were going to buckle.

Then, as if I'd suddenly awakened from a horrible nightmare, I reached up, grabbed the window, and slammed it closed. I grasped the cord dangling from the side, and pulled. The blind fell down and jerked to a stop with an abrupt snapping sound, covering the window. It wavered for a moment, then stilled. Like a television set that had been turned off, the scene beyond my bedroom window vanished.

The house was quiet, except for the loud, frantic *whump-whump, whump-whump* of my heart, thrashing at my rib cage.

Is she gone? I wondered as I stared at the closed blind. *Did I scare her away?* I knew I'd never get to sleep if I Brittany—a vampire—was waiting for me just outside my bedroom window.

After a moment, I reached out and found the cord dangling by the window. I pulled on it, and the blind rose a few inches. I leaned forward carefully and peered outside.

Brittany was gone.

What in the world is going on? I thought. *Is Brittany a vampire?*

No. There's no such thing as vampires. She was just taking the act too far. She wanted so much to be a vampire that she was willing to act out her weird vampire fantasies. Or, maybe she was doing it as a joke, just to scare me. If so, it had worked. I had to admit I had been awfully scared. Maybe I just imagined that I hadn't seen her in the mirror.

My fear faded, and was replaced by the flames of anger.

How dare she? I thought. *How dare she come to my bedroom window in the middle of the night just to scare me, just so she could have her fun?*

Well, I'd get to the bottom of it. I would confront Brittany in school in the morning. At the very least, I would warn her: if she did it again, I would have Mom and Dad call the police. If she did it again, she would be in *big* trouble.

At school the next day, I found Brittany in the lunchroom. She was sitting across the table from Cooper Winneker. Both were eating sandwiches. Brittany used to have brown hair, but she'd recently dyed it black. One of her bangs was dyed a shocking, bright pink, and it curled down her face and around her chin like the blade of a scythe.

"What were you doing at my window last night?" I demanded.

Brittany stopped chewing. She looked at

Cooper, then at me. “What are you talking about?” she asked.

“You know what I’m talking about,” I said. “You came to my bedroom window last night. It was after midnight.”

Brittany shook her head, swallowed a bite of her sandwich, and spoke. “No, I didn’t,” she replied.

“I saw you, and I talked to you,” I said. “It was *you.* I know it was. You wanted me to let you in.”

“You’re weird,” she said, taking another bite of her sandwich.

“You’re the weird one,” I snapped, “dressing up like a vampire and trying to act like one.”

“I can dress any way I want,” Brittany replied.

“But you can’t go around knocking on windows in the middle of the night,” I said. I was really getting angry. “If you do it again, you’re going to be in a lot of trouble.”

I stormed off, mad as ever, hoping Brittany got the message.

As I made my way toward class, I couldn’t help but notice that even more students had acquired the vampire look, and nearly everyone seemed to have a vampire book tucked beneath one arm. One student was actually walking down the hall with his nose in *The Vampire's Mechanic*, and he was reading while he headed toward class. If I hadn't stepped out of his way, he would have run into me.

This is crazy, I thought. This is just getting out of control. Why, all of a sudden, has the vampire craze hit our school? Was it because *Vampire Nation* was so popular?

I had a few minutes before I had to be in class, so I went into the library. I'd finished *The Haunting of Barker's Mansion* during reading time in earlier that morning. It was an excellent book: very spooky and scary. I was going to return it and find another one.

I scoured the shelves. It was getting harder and harder to find any decent scary books that weren't about vampires. They were packed onto every shelf. There must have been hundreds and hundreds of vampire books in the library. Strange.

Finally, I found something that promised to be good: *The Ghost of Silver Bay.* I carried it to the checkout desk, but I didn't see Mrs. Chesapeake. By now, the other students had left. I was alone in the library.

"Mrs. Chesapeake?" I called out. I was certain she was in her office.

Sure enough, I heard some papers rustling and the squeak of a chair.

"Coming," she said, and I was shocked to see Mrs. Chesapeake emerge from her office, dressed in a long, black dress. Her skin was gothic white, and she wore dark lipstick and dark eye liner. She didn't even look like herself anymore.

She smiled as she approached the desk. "Find a good one?" she asked.

"Yeah," I said, trying not to stare. Mrs. Chesapeake is very pretty—she was even very pretty dressed like a vampire. In fact, she looked a lot like Courtney Black, the star of *Vampire Nation*.

But she looked so . . . so *different*.

I handed her the book, and she looked at it. "You'll like this one," she said. "It's excellent. It has an ending that will surprise you. Very creepy."

"That's what I like," I said. "The creepier, the better." I was trying not to stare at her, but Mrs. Chesapeake just looked so odd, so unlike her normal self. I don't know if I was repulsed or fascinated.

She scanned the book and handed it back to me, smiling sweetly. "There you go," she said. "Enjoy. Say . . . isn't it your birthday?"

"Yeah," I said.

"Happy birthday. Are you going to have a party?"

"No," I replied. "But Michelle Adams and I are going to watch the taping of *Vampire Nation* tonight."

Mrs. Chesapeake's eyes lit up. "That'll be fun! I love that show, but I haven't had the time to make it to any of the Fan Nights. You'll have to tell me all about the filming."

"I will," I replied.

I started to walk away, then stopped and turned around.

"Mrs. Chesapeake?" I said.

She looked up from the computer screen. "Yes?"

"I can't help but notice all of the vampire books here in the library," I said. "They're everywhere. It's like there are more and more every day."

"Vampire books sure are popular, aren't they?" she said. "Do you read any?"

I shook my head. "I'm kind of tired of vampire stuff," I said. "It seems like that's all you see or read about anymore."

"And there are more books on the way," Mrs. Chesapeake said. "Everyone is just devouring them. I just ordered a lot more for the library."

As I left, I began to feel frightened, and I didn't know why. I just had a weird sensation, a strange feeling that something was going on, something unseen that wasn't right. It was as if a dark, menacing force was at work, a devious entity slithering through the school like an invisible serpent, circling through the halls and slipping into classrooms, poisoning the air with its unknown presence. It was an eerie feeling, and I couldn't shake it, even after I took my seat in class.

When the bell finally rang and class was dismissed, I made a decision. I decided I would speak to our school counselor about what was going on. Sure, she might think I was crazy, but at the very least, maybe she could reassure me that there was nothing wrong, that it was just my imagination. After all: my mom and dad were always telling me that I have an overactive imagination. Maybe that was it. Perhaps I was just letting my thoughts run a little too wild.

So, while most students were leaving the school to catch their bus or walk home, I went straight to my locker. I pulled out my windbreaker and stored my books. Then, I closed my locker and walked down the hall to the counselor's office.

Mrs. Harper is our school counselor, and she's very nice. I think everyone likes her. She's always smiling, always nodding and saying hello. I don't know her very well, but when I see her in the hall, she always asks how I'm doing and tells me to keep up the good work, that she hears good things about me. Mrs. Harper just has a way of making you feel good.

And I knew she would make me feel better. All I had to do was talk to her, tell her what I was seeing, what I was feeling, what I was thinking. Mrs. Harper would assure me that everything was fine, and I would feel much better.

I knocked on her office door, which creaked open a tiny bit. It hadn't been closed all the way. I saw Mrs. Harper at her desk, her back toward me. She was facing a computer monitor and tapping at a keyboard.

"Mrs. Harper?" I said.

"Just a moment," Mrs. Harper said sweetly, without pausing or turning around. "Come in and sit down."

I pushed the door open, walked into her office, and sat in the chair in front of her desk.

"One more second," she said, tapping furiously. The plastic keys clickety-clacked like popping popcorn. Mrs. Harper sure could type fast.

"There," she said, and she turned her chair to face me.

My skin grew cold, and my scalp felt prickly.

Mrs. Harper was smiling . . . but there was a trickle of blood coming from the side of her mouth, running all the way down to her chin!

6

I thought I was going to explode out of the chair. Seeing the grin on Mrs. Harper's face, and that icicle trickle of blood down her chin was more than I could take. I wanted to run, to get out of the office and away from Mrs. Harper as fast as I could.

But I didn't. I just sat there, staring in horror at the shiny red trickle oozing from her mouth and crawling down her cheek.

Like she's been drinking blood, I thought. *Like she's been feeding on something—or someone.*

Mrs. Harper saw the shocked expression on my face. She nodded, looked at me curiously.

"What's wrong, Amber?" she asked, leaning a little closer. "You look like you've seen a ghost."

Slowly, I raised my arm and pointed to her chin. "There's . . . there's blood on . . . on your chin, Mrs. Harper," I managed to stammer.

Mrs. Harper frowned, puzzled. Then, she turned, plucked a napkin off her desk, and wiped the blood from her chin. She looked at the napkin curiously. Then, her eyes flew open wide, and she laughed.

"This isn't blood," she said. "It's only ketchup." She dropped the napkin in the waste basket, turned once more, and picked up a half-eaten hot dog from a paper plate. Ketchup flooded what was left of the fleshy, pink meat and mushy bun. "I'm having a late lunch," she said. "They had a few leftover hot dogs in the cafeteria. They're not very good, though. Have you ever eaten them?"

I nodded and grimaced. “They taste like rat poison,” I said.

Mrs. Harper laughed again. “Well, I don’t think they’re *that* bad,” she replied. “But, as my mom used to say: it fills the holes.”

“I’d rather eat dirty carpet than cafeteria hot dogs,” I said with a frown. “And don’t eat the pizza, either. It tastes like drywall.”

Mrs. Harper laughed again and drew a warm smile, placing the hot dog and the napkin to the side. “I don’t think you came to see me about cafeteria food,” she said. “How can I help you?”

I told her everything. I told her about the vampire books in the library, about how kids—and some teachers—were dressing like vampires around school. Mrs. Harper listened politely, intently interested in what I had to say. After I finished, she spoke.

“But Amber,” Mrs. Harper said, “you don’t actually *believe* that they’re real vampires, do you?”

“No,” I said, looking at the floor. “I guess not. It just seems weird, that’s all.”

"I think it has a lot to do with that new television series, *Vampire Nation*," she said. "That seems to be a popular show. I read that it's the number one show on TV these days."

"Do you think that's why everyone is reading vampire books and dressing like vampires?" I asked.

"Could be," Mrs. Harper said. "It's probably just a fad. It'll pass in time. And there's nothing wrong with anyone reading about vampires, watching vampire shows, or even dressing like a vampire if they want."

"I guess not," I said. "But . . . ."

My voice trailed off, and I didn't finish the sentence.

Mrs. Harper frowned and gave me a puzzled look. "But what?" she asked.

"Nothing," I said. "Thanks for talking with me."

Mrs. Harper smiled. "That's what I'm here for, sweetheart. You come and see me anytime. Oh . . . and happy birthday. I saw your name on the calendar today."

"Thank you," I said.

I left, and I felt a little better. Not a lot—but a little. Mrs. Harper was right: there was nothing wrong with anyone dressing like a vampire. Maybe if I was a big fan of vampire books or *Vampire Nation*, I might dress that way, too.

But there was something else that bothered me. That night was Fan Night—the taping of the television show—and I'd promised Michelle I would go with her. I really wished I hadn't let her talk me into going. I really didn't want to go, and I knew I'd be bored silly.

Still, I knew I'd learn a lot about how television shows were made, and that would be interesting. It would be cool to see how they put the show together. I told myself that it might be kind of fun, after all.

But I would also learn something else that night. I would learn there really *was* something strange going on, unseen and unknown to anyone, particularly the viewers of *Vampire Nation*. That night, I would discover the truth about the bizarre, horrifying secret that was slowly turning everyone in the country into vampires.

7

Michelle rode her bike to my house after dinner. Together, we cruised through the neighborhood on the sidewalk. I wore my backpack; Mom had given me some money and a small list of a few things she needed from the grocery store, and she'd asked me to pick them up on the way home, after we'd gone to the taping of *Vampire Nation*.

It was October, and the wind was chilly. Michelle and I were both wearing jeans and heavy, warm sweatshirts as we rolled through the neighborhood. Wind whipped our hair that stuck out beneath our helmets. The fall breeze felt like cold steel against my cheeks.

"This is going to be awesome," Michelle said.

"Yeah," I agreed, as we slowed at a busy intersection, then hopped off our bikes and paused to wait for the light to change and traffic to stop, so we could cross the street. A gust of wind tossed my hair over my shoulders and sent cool icicles of air beneath my collar. Directly ahead of us, several blocks away, loomed the huge, gray building that was now a television and movie studio. A bus roared past, spewing a cough of exhaust like an iron dragon.

While we waited for the light to change, a few people—kids, mostly, from our age up to high school age—joined us at the intersection. Most of them were dressed in black, their faces pallid, looking even whiter in contrast to their dark hair. They were probably on their way to the television studio, too.

"*It's not even Halloween, yet,*" I whispered to Michelle, and she giggled.

The light changed and traffic stopped. Michelle and I pushed our bikes through the intersection. The air was crisp and carried the heavy smell of old leaves and chalky automotive exhaust. The sky was flat and ashen, a canopy of curdled gray. Winter was on its way, and with it, even colder air and snow.

As we made our way across the street, I glanced through glossy windshields to see that even some of the drivers and passengers had the look of the undead.

I smiled. Mrs. Harper was right: there was no harm in anyone dressing like a vampire, if that's what they wanted to do. I guess that's a pretty good thing, that we're all able to wear the clothes we want, have the hairstyle and color we want, wear earrings if we want. The world sure would be a boring place if everybody dressed and acted the same.

The enormous building—the television studio—loomed above us like a rectangular mountain, a block of granite beneath a sullen, darkening sky. All of the windows were boarded up, and the building looked abandoned. A few pigeons clapped through the air like feathered bullets, their wings whistling in flight.

Inside the building, however, the atmosphere was completely different. After we'd locked our bikes and helmets to a light pole, we followed a line of people through two large double doors, down a long hallway, and finally through another series of double doors that opened into a very large room resembling a movie theater without the screen. The air was clean and fresh-smelling, like new leather and saddle soap. There were rows and rows of shiny, black seats with plush, cherry-red cushions. In front, a wide balcony overlooked a large stage on the lower floor. On the stage were several sets: three separate rooms, one of which contained furniture: chairs, tables, and lamps. There was a room that was obviously a kitchen, as it had a stove, refrigerator, sink, and a table with four empty dining chairs seated around it. Another room looked like an attic, and there was a long, dark coffin in it. All around the stage, there were several large tripods supporting bulky cameras. Above, the ceiling was a shadowy, spider web network of dangling wires, wrapped cables, knotted cords, can lights, and more cameras. While the outside of the building might not be much to look at—abandoned, in fact—everything inside appeared to be new.

The polished, deep voice of a man came through unseen speakers, reminding me of our principal when he read the school's morning announcements.

"Ladies and gentlemen, please be seated. Welcome to Fan Night, and the taping of *Vampire Nation*. The cast and crew are on break, but will be resuming work in just a few minutes. Meanwhile, here are a few reminders . . . ."

The voice droned on smoothly, saying that no smoking was allowed, no applause or talking while the taping was in progress, turn off all phones and pagers . . . stuff like that. Michelle and I both pulled out our phones and set our ring tones to vibrate.

Below us, on the stage, people were appearing: camera operators and crew members. Then, some of the main characters of *Vampire Nation* strode onto the stage. It was kind of exciting, even if I didn't follow the show or know who the characters were. I did recognize Courtney Black, though. She was tall and willowy, with gallons of glossy, black hair cascading over her shoulders and down her back. She looked just like she did in the magazines.

All around the viewing theater, electricity filled the air. It seemed liked everyone in the audience wanted to clap their hands, but no one did.

Although we could see what was going on, we couldn't hear the characters very well. The microphones they were using were big, tube-like things covered with dark foam and were out of camera range, so they wouldn't be seen on television. But those microphones were strictly for recording purposes, not for use over a speaker system.

Still, it was interesting. They filmed the scenes in bits and pieces. Some scenes only lasted only a couple of minutes; others were longer. The characters changed sets, moving from the living room to the dining room. Occasionally, one of the actors or actresses would mess up their lines and everyone would laugh, and they'd begin that particular scene again.

"They do all the fancy stuff—you know, the stunts and things—in another part of the building," Michelle whispered as she turned her head and leaned closer to me. *"They don't allow studio audiences to watch."*

"But don't they do some of the filming outside?" I asked quietly.

Michelle nodded. *"They don't allow people to watch during those, either, unless you're invited. And to get—"*

My phone suddenly vibrated in my pocket.

"Hang on," I whispered, cutting off Michelle in mid-sentence. I plucked the phone from my pocket and looked at the glowing display screen.

Mom.

"It's my Mom," I whispered as I got up. *"I have to answer. I'll be right back."*

I hustled up the aisle to the back of the theater, looking for someplace private where I could talk with my mom and not disturb anyone in the audience . . . or the taping of the show.

At the back of the theater, there was a sign that read *RESTROOMS,* and, beneath it, a set of double doors.

As good of a place as any, I thought.

The phone was still vibrating in my hand as I pushed through the doors and into a long hallway. I put the phone to my ear, just as the doors closed behind me.

"Hi, Mom," I said, continuing to walk down the hall as I spoke. The restrooms were at the end of the hall, but there were a few doors on each side of the hallway. All of them were closed, but one was open a tiny bit. I could hear someone—a man—speaking in the room when I walked past. A sign above the door read: *PRODUCTION STUDIO* in bold letters. Beneath it: *Mr. Lou Turndacca, Executive Producer.*

"Hi, Ambs," Mom said. She calls me that a lot. "How are things?"

"Good," I replied quietly. "I'm at the taping of *Vampire Nation*."

"I won't keep you. Can you add something to my grocery list?"

"Sure," I said. "What else do you need." I continued walking down the hall.

"Mustard. We're completely out."

"Sure."

" Have fun, and I'll see you in a little while. Love you."

"Love you, too, Mom. Bye."

I stopped walking, stuffed the phone into my back pocket, and was about to hurry back to watch the taping. But as I passed by the production studio door, a deep, oily voice caught my attention.

". . . won't be long now," a man was saying. He had a strong, foreign accent. "When the final episode of the season airs, the mutation process will be complete. Everyone who has been watching the show will be transformed into a vampire."

A cold chill needled my body. I know it's wrong to eavesdrop, to listen to other people's private conversations, but I couldn't help myself. What the man said was horrifying, and I couldn't tear myself away. I leaned close and peered through the tiny crack of the partially-opened door.

A man with his back to me sat at a long desk that appeared to be one gigantic piece of equipment. There were switches and buttons and sliders and dials and lights. There were several computer monitors on other desks, most of them displaying the frozen scene of what I assumed was an episode of *Vampire Nation*. The man was holding a small phone to his ear. He had thick, silver hair that shined like chrome fibers under the bright florescent lights, and he was dressed in black. In front of him, a large computer screen glowed.

"That's right," he continued. "When I produce the show, I place computer-generated, subliminal sounds within the episodes. Humans can't hear the sounds, but their brain waves pick them up."

Subliminal? I thought. I knew what the word meant, as it had been on a recent spelling test at school. It meant 'below conscious perception,' meaning, of course, that no one could hear the sounds.

He paused for a moment, and I told myself to leave. I was spying, and I knew it. It wasn't right.

But what the man was saying was terrifying. What did he mean when he said that everyone who had watched the show would turn into vampires after the last episode of the season?

"Yes," he began again. "No one suspects a thing. Everyone who has been watching episodes of *Vampire Nation* has slowly been turning. There are some—the younger, weaker ones—who have already turned."

Brittany! I thought, remembering how she'd been at my window the night before. *Maybe she'd really turned into a vampire!*

Lou Turndacca continued speaking. "By the time the final episode airs, everyone who has been watching will be a vampire. Those who haven't been watching? Well, we'll rule them soon enough."

He paused for another moment, listening to the phone pressed to his ear, then continued. "That's right. All of the shows are produced here, in the studio, and are saved on a computer. We feed the show directly to the network through a satellite hookup. No one suspects a thing."

Then, the man laughed, deep and gravelly, like rock scraping rock.

Finally, I mustered enough willpower to flee. There was something in his sinister laughter, something vile and sickening. I had to get away from that awful sound. I wanted it out of my ears, out of my head.

I spun quietly on my heels, ready to bolt down the hall and into the theater . . . but I didn't get very far. I was stopped by a tall, blue-uniformed security officer. He stood in the middle of the hallway, hands on his hips. His skin was a supple, glue-white, and his lips parted to form an evil grin . . . displaying two sharp fangs at each corner of his mouth!

8

The security guard looked at me for a moment, then took a cautious step to the side of the hall. He was still grinning, but only slightly. I could no longer see his fangs.

"Problem, Miss?" he asked. His eyes were penetrating, searching. *Did he know I had been eavesdropping?*

"Um, no," I replied. "I was just talking to my mom on the phone, and I didn't want to interrupt anyone in the theater."

He continued staring into my eyes, and I wondered if he believed me. I wondered if I was going to get into trouble.

"Better hurry back," he said, with a leering grin. He waved his arm slowly, motioning for me to continue down the hall. "Hurry along, or you'll miss the best part."

I exhaled and walked past him, watching him out of the corner of my eye, thinking that he might, at any moment, lunge out, grab me, and bite my neck . . . but he didn't. I hustled down the hall, and soon I was pushing through the big double doors and wading through the foggy darkness of the theater to my seat. I took my place next to Michelle, watching the bustle of activity below on the stage, but the only thing I could think about was what that awful man had said in the production studio.

By the time the final episode airs, everyone who has been watching will be a vampire.

Was it possible?

Those who haven't been watching? Well, we'll rule them soon enough.

It was totally crazy. It was totally crazy, and there was no way I was going to believe it.

By the time the final episode airs, everyone who has been watching will be a vampire.

No way.

Those who haven't been watching? Well, we'll rule them soon enough.

No matter what I told myself, I couldn't get the man's heavy, clotted voice and his horrifying words out of my head.

"Amber?"

Michelle had gotten to her feet, along with the rest of the audience. The house lights came on. I had been so caught up in my own thoughts that I didn't even know that the filming was over, that people were getting up.

"Want to stay for a few minutes and see if any of the stars come out to sign autographs?" Michelle asked.

"No," I said, shaking my head. "I've got to tell you some—"

I stopped. I was about to tell Michelle about what I'd overheard, and about the strange security guard with the sharp, pointed teeth . . . but I decided not to. She'd think I was looney.

"You've got to tell me what?" Michelle asked.

"Oh, nothing. It's just that I've got to get to the store and get some groceries for Mom. We'd better get going."

Outside, we unlocked our bikes and put our helmets on.

"Well," Michelle said as she hopped onto her bike, "I'll see you tomorrow at school."

"See ya," I said.

At the grocery store, I pulled out Mom's grocery list and picked up a blue basket by the front door. It only took me only a few minutes to get the things she needed. I was making my way toward the cashier, skirting through the vegetable aisle, when I saw something that caught eye.

I stopped.

Picked it up. Picked up another one.

I held the two items in my hand with reverence, like I was holding an expensive piece of china. The dark words of Lou Turndacca, the show's Executive Producer, drifted into my head like a heavy cloud.

Those who haven't been watching? Well, we'll rule them soon enough.

I stared at the items for another moment, then dropped them in the blue basket. It wouldn't hurt to have a couple, just in case.

On my way home, I started getting a bad feeling about things. Night was quickly approaching, and the sky was a cheerless, dark gray membrane. The air seemed colder than ever, and the wind snuck through my sweatshirt and chilled my skin. I rode past a few people, and most of them were dressed all in black, their exposed skin the color of ivory, nearly glowing in the coming night.

Something really is wrong, I thought. *As impossible as it seems, as crazy as it sounds, maybe what Lou Turndacca said is true. Maybe people really are turning into vampires. Maybe it's not an act.*

I was confused. I thought the only way people turned into vampires was if they had been bitten by one. At least, that's the way it was in all the books and movies. Who ever heard of subliminal sounds in a television show turning humans into the living dead?

I rounded the corner and turned onto my street. The streetlights were on, creating angular domes of flour-colored light. Windows were lit, forming warm squares and rectangles. Several porch lights were burning. A car idled in a driveway, its red taillights glowing like embers.

But there were no lights on in my house. Not one. It sat outcast and alone, black and uninviting among the other well-lit homes.

That feeling hit me again, harder, heavier, pressing down upon my shoulders. Something was wrong. Something was very, very wrong. There was venom in the air, something rotten and unclean. I could feel it on my flesh and in my bones.

I rode up the dark driveway, hopped off my bike, and leaned it against the house. I took my helmet off and hung it on the bicycle seat. My backpack filled with Mom's groceries was on my back, and I slipped it off, carrying it with my right hand as I walked up the porch steps.

At the door, I stopped.

Listened.

Not a single sound. No television, no talking. Nothing.

Where is everyone? I wondered. *What is going on?*

Even the doorknob seemed abnormally cold. Chilly.

I turned the knob and pushed the door open. The living room was dark.

"Mom?" I called out. "Dad?"

I was getting really scared. It wasn't like Mom or Dad to be gone in the evening. Dad is on a Monday night bowling league . . . but this was Wednesday. He should be home. Everyone should be home.

"Mom? Dad? Brent?"

I listened.

And when I reached over and flipped the light switch, chaos and madness broke loose.

9

The shock of suddenly seeing so many people in the living room frightened me so much that I dropped my backpack on the floor. My hands flew to my mouth. People had been hiding behind chairs, the couch, in the kitchen, and in the closet. When I flipped the light switch, they all jumped up and leapt out at once.

"Surprise!" they shouted in unison.

Everyone was wearing party hats. A banner on the wall read 'HAPPY BIRTHDAY, AMBER!' in gold foil letters. Mom came out of the kitchen with a glazed white birthday cake with thin, unlit candles of blue, red, yellow, and green. Everyone had noisemakers—kazoos, little clappers, horns—and the room was filled with laughter and a cacophony of riotous, festive sounds. Standing by the couch was Michelle. She was wearing a silver, cone-shaped hat. It was secured to her head by a thin, elastic band running behind her ear and beneath her chin. My brother, Brent, was wearing the same kind of hat, grinning.

I smiled as everyone began to sing 'Happy Birthday.' Dad lit the candles on the cake, and as the song ended, I made a wish and blew them out. Everyone clapped and cheered.

"You guys really surprised me," I said.

"That's why they're called 'surprise parties,'" said Michelle.

"You knew about this all along?" I asked her.

Michelle nodded. "Your mom asked me to do something to get you out of the house tonight," she said. "They needed time to get the party ready without you knowing about it. Being that it was Fan Night for *Vampire Nation*, I thought it would be perfect."

Mom carried the cake into the kitchen, followed by Dad. "We'll have the cake cut in just a minute," he said. "Napkins and plates are on the table. Everyone can help themselves. We have pizza, too."

I looked around the room. Besides my family and Michelle, there were a few other friends from school and some of Brent's friends. Even Cooper Winneker was there, dressed in black, his skin an unhealthy white sheen. There were a few others that were dressed in black and looked the same.

I shrugged it off. They were friends, and I didn't care how they dressed or what they acted like. It was no big deal.

Lou Turndacca's voice echoed in my mind.

By the time the final episode airs, everyone who has been watching will be a vampire.

No. Can't be true.

Those who haven't been watching? Well, we'll rule them soon enough.

Impossible.

I pushed the voice out of my head, and let myself get carried away with the party. Everyone ate cake, chattered, and laughed. I opened presents. Mom and Dad had bought me some new clothes. Michelle bought me a book called *The Official Guide to Real Haunted Houses.* Brent gave me a gift certificate to the music store, which was cool.

And we had fun. I talked with everyone and thanked them for coming. We laughed and ate birthday cake and pizza. Mom brought out a game—Twister—and we had hilarious fun with it.

Sometime during the evening, Mom had picked up my backpack and carried it into the kitchen. Now, she came into the living room with a puzzled look on her face while we were playing Twister. On the mat of colorful, large dots, Michelle's body was arched in a ridiculously funny pose, and we were all laughing and watching, waiting for her to collapse.

I looked up. Mom was carrying the two extra items I'd bought at the grocery store—the ones I'd picked up in the vegetable aisle—and she held them out.

Garlic.

Two bulbs, each the size of a golf ball.

"Why did you buy these, Amber?" Mom asked.

Heads turned. Suddenly, without a word, several people shot to their feet. They hustled through the living room and out the front door. Even my brother, Brent, sprang to his feet and raced outside.

Mom was dumbfounded. She held the two garlic bulbs in her hand, an expression of puzzled shock on her face. "What was that all about?" she asked as she nodded toward the front door.

Vampires don't like garlic, I thought with a shudder. I'd forgotten all about buying the two bulbs at the grocery store. I'd bought them just in case—*just in case*—what Lou Turndacca said was true.

"They didn't even say good-bye," Michelle said. She, too, was confused.

"Maybe it was time for them to go," Mom said. "They sure left in a hurry." Then, she asked me again: "Amber . . . what did you buy these for?"

I hesitated for a moment. *What am I going to do?* I thought. *Tell her I bought them to ward off bloodthirsty vampires? She and Dad would think I was cracking up.*

"I . . . I guess I thought you needed them for something," I stammered.

Mom shrugged. "Well, no harm in having a little extra garlic around. Thanks." She returned to the kitchen.

It was getting later, and it was a school night. The rest of my friends said good-bye, and left. I gave Michelle a hug and thanked her for the book.

"That was really strange," she said. "When your mom came into the room, some people freaked out and left."

It wasn't my mom, I thought. *It was the garlic. They—*

The vampires?

—don't like garlic.

"Be careful walking home," I said, and my words sounded strange, foreign.

Michelle frowned. "Why?" she asked. "I only live a couple blocks away."

"Just . . . just be careful, that's all," I said.

"I'll be fine, Amber. See you in the morning."

She left, and I closed the front door behind her.

"Where's Brent?" Mom asked from the kitchen.

"He went outside a while ago," I said, and I walked through the living room and stood in the hall, looking into the kitchen. Dad was at the table, reading a newspaper and eating a piece of birthday cake. Mom was putting the two garlic bulbs in her spice drawer.

Lou Turndacca's voice slid into my head again.

By the time the final episode airs, everyone who has been watching will be a vampire.

"Mom," I said. "There's—"

I stopped speaking, and Mom turned and smiled. "Yes?"

"Never mind," I said. "I'm going to bed. Thanks for the great party and the birthday gifts."

"I'll come tuck you in after I pick up a few things," Mom said.

I rolled my eyes. "I don't need to be tucked in," I said.

While I was brushing my teeth, I heard the front door open and bang close. Brent was home. As I climbed into bed, I could hear him talking with Mom and Dad in the living room. He said he'd only gone outside to find out what was wrong with some of his friends, why they had left in such a hurry.

"It was weird how they just got up and took off like that," I heard him say. "Like they were scared of something."

But was my brother telling the truth? I wondered as I lay back in bed. *Maybe my brother was scared away by the garlic, just like the other—*

Vampires.

Was he?

Was he one of . . . *them?* My own *brother?*

Sure, he didn't watch *Vampire Nation* a lot, but maybe just a few episodes were all it took. Even though he didn't dress in black and his face wasn't white, maybe he, too, was slowly turning.

Mutation, I thought. *That's the word that Lou Turndacca had used. Maybe Brent was slowly mutating.*

If he was, and if what Lou Turndacca said was true, my own brother was in danger of becoming a full-fledged, un-dead creature of the night.

A vampire.

Later that night, I had a horrible dream. In it, my brother had appeared in my bedroom doorway, flashing two razor-sharp fangs. All I could see was his black silhouette. His arms were open wide, only they weren't arms, but rather what appeared to be wings. His eyes burned red, and he was hissing like an angry cat. It was such a terrifying scene that I awoke with a jolt and snapped upright. My skin was hot, and I was sweating.

Just a dream, I thought, as I lay back and pulled the covers up to my chin.

Still, I wondered.

Was my very own brother slowly turning into a vampire?

There was one way to find out. If Brent really *was* turning into a vampire, I had to know. I didn't know if there was anything I could do about it, but I had to *know*.

Slowly, quietly, I slipped out of bed, tiptoed out of my room, down the hall, and into the kitchen. It was dark, but the blue neon glow of the clock on the stove cast an eerie, dreamy light, enough for me to see. The cold tile chilled my bare feet as I walked to the counter. I found Mom's spice drawer, pulled out the two garlic bulbs, and silently made my way through the kitchen, back down the hall, stopping at Brent's bedroom. His door was open halfway.

I poked my head in. His room was hollow and dark, silent as a tomb. Cold, even.

Strange.

I held the two bulbs of garlic in my left hand, and, with my right, I flipped on the bedroom light switch.

The brightness was nearly overwhelming, and it hurt my eyes. I squinted.

A creeping terror snaked up my spine as my mind grasped the reality—the absolute horror—of what I was seeing and what it meant.

Brent was not in his bed . . . and his window was open.

10

I stood in his bedroom, shivering. The cream-colored window curtain, which was open and drawn to the side of the window, billowed gently like a lonely ghost.

I peered through the open window and looked out into the neighborhood. Streetlights cast an ominous, forbidding glow over houses, yards, and parked cars. The road was a dark, gray river, and the grass in our yard shined with a thin glaze of icy frost. Nothing moved except the curtain.

And I knew.

It's true, I thought. *Everything Lou Turndacca said was true. The television show*—Vampire Nation—*was turning people into vampires. My brother—my very own brother—has become like them. He's a creature of the night, and he's out there, right now, somewhere.*

My mind was reeling. Brent's room seemed to tilt and spin before my eyes, and I placed one hand against the wall to keep myself steady. I felt dizzy, nauseous.

Vampire Nation *is the most popular television series on the air,* I thought. *How many hundreds of thousands—how many millions of people—watch the show every week? The last episode is only six days away. In a few days, everyone who watches the season finale of* Vampire Nation *will join the legions of the un-dead. Through some sort of strange process generated by a computer and fed through the sound waves of the television show, people will become full-fledged vampires.*

I sat on Brent's bed, wondering what to do. Who could I tell? Who could stop Lou Turndacca? My parents? They would send me to the looney bin. If I started telling them that the televison show was turning ordinary people into monsters, they would think I'd flipped my lid.

The police? Same thing. If I told the police about it, they would never believe me.

Think, Amber. Think.

The air drifting through Brent's open bedroom window was frigid, and my skin had broken out in gooseflesh. I stood and closed the window, pausing to stare out into the yard, the road, and the houses across the street.

Something moved.

A dark shape moved near a bush next to the house directly across from ours. I was sure of it.

I watched. My heart beat faster, my breaths came quicker.

There. It moved again. A shadow against the house. There was something there, concealed in the bushes.

Then, the creature showed itself, and I let out a sigh of relief. It was only a cat, slinking around in the bushes. Its shadow on the side of the house made it look bigger, like it had been something else.

I sat again, forcing myself to think. My mind replayed the scene at the television studio, from the moment I stopped at the door of the production room, listening to the awful, deep voice of Lou Turndacca. I tried to remember everything he'd said, what he was explaining to someone over the phone. I thought about what I could do, who I could tell.

How can he be stopped?

And the more I thought about it, the more I realized that I would have to tell Mom and Dad. After all: it was the middle of the night, and Brent was gone. He had no business climbing out the window and leaving the house after dark. Of course, that's what vampires do, I supposed. Still, Mom and Dad would be worried sick, and they would want to find him.

Tell Mom and Dad, I told myself. *At the very least, tell them Brent is gone. That would be the right thing to do.*

I stood. Still holding the garlic bulbs in my hand, I walked out of Brent's bedroom and into the hallway.

At the end of the hall was the dark figure of a person, slowly coming toward me.

My brother.

He was coming toward me, slowly, his head down.

And he was speaking quietly, in a voice that didn't even seem his own.

"*Thirsty,*" he said. "*So . . . thirsty . . . .*"

11

I tried to scream, but my tongue knotted, and the sound caught in my throat and stayed there. My mouth remained open in a silent, terrified gasp.

Brent suddenly saw me, and he flinched and stopped in the middle of the hall. He hadn't seen me standing there, and I'd surprised him.

"What are you doing?" he hissed sleepily. *"And why is my bedroom light on?"*

I didn't answer. Instead, I held out the garlic

bulbs for him to see, carefully watching his reaction.

He came closer, reached out, and plucked both garlic bulbs from my hand.

"What's this?" he asked. *"A midnight snack? You're going to have some awful breath in the morning."* He handed the garlic bulbs back to me.

"You . . . you're not afraid of garlic?" I stammered quietly.

"Why?" he asked. *"Do you think I'm a vampire, or something? What were you doing in my bedroom?"*

"What are you doing out of bed?" I whispered.

"I had to use the bathroom, and I'm thirsty, so now I'm going to the kitchen to get a glass of water."

"Why is your bedroom window open? And why were you talking to yourself?" I asked.

"I was hot, that's why," Brent said. *"I always open my window if my room gets too warm. And I wasn't talking to myself. I was just mumbling."*

"I have to talk to you about something," I said. *"Get your glass of water, and I'll wait for you in your bedroom."*

Brent gave me a strange look. *"What's so*

important that you have to tell me in the middle of the night?" he asked.

"Get your water," I replied, *"and I'll tell you."*

In Brent's bedroom, I told him everything I knew. He was, of course, aware of the many people who had been dressing up like vampires.

"I have noticed," he said, "that more and more people every day are dying their hair black and dressing strange. Even some of my friends. I've been thinking how weird it is. And some teachers at school are dressing like vampires."

"Earlier tonight," I said, "when Mom came into the living room with the garlic,"—I again showed him the bulbs in my hand—"some people really freaked out. Even *you* ran from the room."

"I just wanted to see what was going on with my friends," Brent replied. "I thought that was a strange thing for them to do, to run outside like that."

"I know that, now," I said. "But Brent, think about it: they were afraid of garlic. I thought *you* were afraid of garlic, too. That's why I had to know, for sure, tonight. I had to know if garlic had any effect on you."

And when I told him what Lou Turndacca, the Executive Producer had said, Brent didn't think I was crazy. He listened with concentrated fascination, his eyes wide and absorbing, paying close attention until I'd finished speaking.

"That's whacked out," he said finally.

"So . . . you believe me?" I asked.

"It seems pretty crazy," Brent said. "But I guess, in a strange way, it makes sense. That would explain why so many people are dressing like vampires. Who else knows this?"

I shook my head. "I don't know. You're the first I've told. I know Mom and Dad will never believe me. I'm sure not many people will."

"This is like something out of a horror movie," Brent said. "Or one of my comic books."

"It's a lot worse than that," I replied. "It's a hundred times worse than any movie or comic, because it's real. It's happening all around us, in Flint, and all across the country, wherever *Vampire Nation* is televised. What are we going to do?"

"The only thing we *can* do," Brent said. "We

have to stop him."

I stared at him. "How?" I said. My voice sounded desperate, unhopeful. "We're a couple of kids. What can we do to stop someone—or something—that might not even be human? After all, if he's a vampire, he's not even among the living. What are we supposed to do? Chase him down with a wooden stake?"

"We've got to use our heads," Brent said. "We have to think of a way to stop him. There must be something we can do to stop the airing of the season finale of *Vampire Nation*. If I can get my hands on his computer, we might be able to do something."

I hadn't thought about that. Brent was a whiz at computers. Maybe there was something we *could* do, after all.

"Well," I said, "there's nothing we can do about it tonight. Let's sleep on it and see what we can come up with in the morning."

I returned to my bedroom, but before I climbed into bed, I opened the blind just a crack and peered out the window.

They're out there, somewhere, I thought. *The un-dead. Creatures of the night. They're out there, maybe on the other side of the street, lurking in the shadows.* I looked up. *Maybe up there, sailing through the sky on nimble, dark wings.*

My sleep was troubled. Bizarre images kept flashing into my head, disturbing my slumber. Images of fangs, of strange, winged creatures. I tossed and turned all night long, wondering who, among my friends was slowly turning into vampires. All along, I'd thought it was an act. I had no idea that they were *really* turning into the un-dead.

In the morning, I lay in bed for a long time, thinking, staring at the ceiling, wondering what we could do to stop Lou Turndacca and his awful plan.

Brent is right, I thought. *The key to stopping him is through his computer.*

Finally, I got out of bed, put on my slippers, and walked into the kitchen. Mom stood at the sink. Her back was to me.

"Hi, Mom," I yawned.

Mom turned, and I recoiled at the sight of her, at the sudden shock of what I was seeing. My yawn became a muted gasp, and my hands flew to my face and covered my mouth.

The robed creature standing in the kitchen wasn't my mother. If she was, she'd changed. She looked like my mother in every other way, except her face.

Her face had gone completely white! My mom—my very own mother—was becoming a vampire!

12

I stood at the edge of the kitchen, my breath hitching, coming in fits and gasps. I felt like I'd been punched in the stomach, and a knot in my belly tightened like a noose.

My mother, seeing my expression and behavior, frowned. "Oh, for goodness' sake, Amber," she said. "It's not that bad. It's just a moisturizing mask on my face. I know it looks a little scary, but you'll do the same thing when you get older."

"A . . . a mask?" I stuttered.

"It's just a cream I put on my face," Mom replied, returning to her work at the sink. "In ten minutes, I'll rinse it off. It makes my skin smoother."

"It freaked me out," I said. "I thought you were a vampire."

Mom laughed. "Not hardly," she said. "Want some breakfast?"

"Yeah," I said. " But I can get it."

While I was eating a bowl of cereal, Brent came in, groggy and sleepy. He poured himself a bowl of cornflakes and sat at the table. When Mom left the kitchen, he turned to me.

"I've got an idea," he whispered as he munched his cereal.

"You do?" I replied quietly. *"Really?"*

He nodded as he scooped a spoonful of cereal. *"Yeah. But I need to get into that guy's computer, and we might need one more person as a lookout."*

"Michelle Adams," I said. *"She'll help. I know she will. Especially if she knows what is going on."*

"Let's talk to her in school this morning," Brent

said. *"We'll fill her in on what's going on, and see if she can help us. Then—"*

Mom suddenly came into the kitchen, causing Brent to stop speaking. I was startled once again by her stark-white face. Whatever the cream was supposed to do, I couldn't see myself putting any of it on my own face, and certainly not walking around the house where my family could see.

"And what are you two whispering about?" Mom asked playfully, like we were discussing a secret joke or prank.

"Oh, you know," Brent said. "Vampires. We're trying to figure out how to stop an evil guy from turning everyone in the country into vampires."

I glared at my brother in disbelief. I couldn't believe he said that.

"Well," Mom said, "whatever you do, I hope it works. I have no desire to become a vampire. That doesn't sound very fun at all."

"Probably not," Brent said confidently. "But I'm sure we'll have it under control."

"Good," Mom said. "And while you're at it, take care of any pesky werewolves you see."

"You got it," Brent replied, and he winked at me as he shoveled another spoonful of cornflakes into his mouth. I shook my head and rolled my eyes.

Before I went to school, I took one of the garlic bulbs and stuffed it in my coat pocket. I wasn't taking any chances. I figured if there were real vampires walking around, it would be smart to have some protection.

Later, in the school lunchroom, Brent and I sat with Michelle, explaining what was going on. She listened with rapt attention, her eyes going from me to Brent, back to me, then to Brent. We told her all about Lou Turndacca, the evil Executive Producer, and what I'd overheard. I told her about Brittany Collins, and how she had come to my bedroom window after midnight, wanting me to invite her inside.

"You think this is really happening around us?" she asked, looking around the cafeteria. "Are people really turning into vampires?"

I shook my head. "Not everyone," I said. "But soon. When the last episode of *Vampire Nation* airs, everyone who has been following the series will be completely turned. They'll be vampires."

"And what happens to the rest of us?" Michelle asked.

"Whatever it is, it can't be good," I replied. "Think about it: our whole lives will change. If we live in a country full of vampires, we'll always have to be on guard, watching for them all the time. We might even have to go into hiding. It'll be horrible."

"*Vampire Nation* is the most popular television series on the air," Michelle said. "Millions of people watch it every week."

"That's what I'm saying," I said. "This is worse than anyone could ever imagine."

"But what can we do about it?" Michelle asked.

"We have an idea," Brent said. "But we need your help."

"I'm not sure I like the sound of that," Michelle said. Her eyes met mine, then returned to Brent. "What are you thinking?"

My brother shared his plan, and told Michelle that he wanted her to come along and act as a lookout.

"Do you really think it will work?" Michelle said, after he'd finished.

"Yeah," Brent said with a nod. "But it's going to take three of us. You guys are going to need to watch out for that creepy guy while I get into his computer."

"And what if we fail?" Michelle asked.

I looked at Brent, and he looked at me. Then, he looked at Michelle. "We can't fail," he said.

Michelle was silent for a moment. The lunch bell rang; it was time to return to class.

"Okay," she said, getting to her feet. "I'll help. But we'd better not get into trouble."

"We won't," Brent said, standing up. "We'll be fine."

"Really?" Michelle said. "Do you really believe that, for sure?"

A look of serious concern, a dark shadow, fell over Brent's face.

"No," was all he said.

13

The odds were against us . . . that's all there was to it.

"Are you sure there's nothing else we can do?" I asked. Brent, Michelle, and I were walking home from school. It was another overcast day, the sky a dusky, mouse gray. The clouds were flat, merged together, as if laminated into a single canvas. On the trees, most of the leaves had turned brown and fallen from their branches. They skirted and scratched across the pavement like paper claws, tossed about by a cold, bitter wind. That same chilly air gnawed at my face, and I was glad I was wearing my coat.

Brent dug his hands into his front pockets to keep them warm. "Well," he said, "there's nothing we can do to stop the taping. Besides: the television show isn't the problem. The problem is that dude Turndacca and the sound waves that are being sent from the computer to the satellite. We have to stop the final episode of *Vampire Nation'* from being broadcast."

"Or go to the police and have the producer arrested," Michelle said.

"That would be best," I said, "but who's going to believe us?"

"Nobody, that's who," Brent said. "That's why we're going to do something about it. We're going to have to somehow stop the show from being sent to the satellite, or stop the guy from putting the hidden sound waves in the recorded episode. Or disable his computer."

"Easier said than done," I said.

We stopped in front of Michelle's house, and I spoke.

"Let's do it tonight," I said. "After dinner. We'll go to the movie studio and see if we can get inside."

"You mean, like, sneak in?" Michelle asked.

Brent shook his head. "No," he said. "But maybe we can talk our way in. You know—convince the security guard that we'd like to get an autograph or something."

"I could tell him that I'm working on my report for school!" Michelle said.

Brent nodded. "We can try. Meet us at our house at six o'clock."

As it turned out, there was no way the security guard was going to let us in.

Michelle met us at our house at six, and we rode our bikes to the studio. A large man with a thick, blue jacket and a blue hat stood by the door. We hopped off our bikes, locked them to a light pole in the parking lot, and took off our helmets.

"Let's see if he'll let us in," I said, after we'd hung our helmets on our bikes. We strode across the parking lot and approached the security guard.

"Hi," I said.

"Hello," the security guard replied. His voice was deep and smooth, a radio announcer's voice. On his coat was the word SECURITY stitched in yellow letters. Beneath it was a silver badge with the name *Charles LeVille* engraved on it.

"We know it's not Fan Night," Michelle said, "but we were hoping we could get inside, just for a few minutes. I'm doing a report on how television shows are made, and it's due tomorrow."

The security guard shook his head. "I'm sorry," he replied. "But I can't let you in. Wish I could bend the rules for you, but I can't. Sorry."

"Just for a few minutes?" she asked.

"No," the security guard replied. "Like I said: I wish I could bend the rules for you, but I've got strict orders."

"Thanks anyway," Michelle said.

The security guard nodded, and we walked away.

"At least he was nice about it," said Brent.

"Let's go around back," I said. "There might be another door. Maybe we can find a different security guard who will let us in."

We hiked around the massive building. In the back, there were about fifty cars parked; a few semi trucks with trailers; and several long, black limousines, polished and shiny like metal beetles.

"I'll bet the stars of *Vampire Nation* ride in those," I said.

The words had just escaped from my mouth when the driver's door of one of the limousines opened. A tall man emerged, wearing a black suit with a white shirt, and black tie. He walked along the side of the limousine and opened a door at the back of the vehicle. He stood, very official-like, holding the door open.

And who should step out of the limousine? Courtney Black, the star of *Vampire Nation*! She was only thirty feet from us! Although I'd never watched the show, I'd seen her on the covers of magazines. Seeing her for real, up close, was exciting. She was just as pretty—maybe more so—than her pictures.

The limousine driver closed the door, and Courtney began walking toward the back of the building . . . and that's when Michelle took action.

"Miss Black!" she said.

The actress turned and stopped. She looked at us and smiled. Her long, black hair tossed and swirled in the breeze.

"Yes?" she replied.

Michelle began to walk toward the actress, and Brent and I followed.

"I'm sorry to bother you," Michelle said, "but—"

"—you'd like an autograph?" Courtney Black said as she reached up into her coat and produced a gold pen.

"Well, yes," Michelle replied. "But also something else." She pleaded her case about how she was working on a report for school, that it had to be finished by the next day, and she needed to get in to watch the taping of the show and maybe talk to some of the crew.

Courtney Black smiled. "Well, tonight's taping is closed to the public," she said. "But since you're doing this for a school project, I'll see to it that you can come in." She looked at Brent, then me. "How about you two? Are you doing a report, too?"

"I am now," I said.

"Yeah, me, too," Brent chimed.

I looked incredulously at my brother, and he looked at me. I couldn't believe I was standing in a parking lot with Courtney Black, the star of *Vampire Nation* . . . and she was inviting us to watch the taping!

"Follow me," Courtney said, and she led the way to a large, gray door where a security officer stood.

"Evening, Miss Black," the officer said, nodding.

"Hello, Frank," the actress replied. "These three young friends are my guests tonight. Could you call my assistant and have him issue passes to each of them?"

"We get our own passes!" Michelle whispered with a squeal of delight.

A small phone appeared in the security guard's hand. "Right away, Miss Black," he said as he pressed the phone to his ear. With his free hand, he opened the door, and we followed Courtney Black inside, through a long corridor. At the end of the hall, a man stood by an open door. When we approached, he stood aside and let us through. I recognized where we were right away: we were on the stage where they filmed the show. Several crew members scurried about, adjusting this and that, chatting to one another. Most of them wore headsets with a thin microphone that curved down to their mouths.

"I've got to get to my dressing room," Courtney said. "But Gabe, my assistant, will—oh, there he is now."

A sharply dressed man wearing a gray suit walked toward us. He had thick, blonde hair. His eyes were a rich, glacial shade of blue. "Good evening, Courtney," he said pleasantly. He was carrying three plastic squares, each the size of an average postcard. Attached to the cards were thin, black cords.

"Hello, Gabe," Courtney said. "These three students are my guests this evening. They are doing reports for school, and might have a few questions. Could you show them your hospitality?"

Gabe nodded. "Certainly."

"It was a pleasure meeting the three of you," Courtney Black said as she glanced at each one of us. We took turns shaking her hand, and she walked off.

"I'm never washing this hand again, ever," Michelle said, staring at her palm in wonder and amazement.

"Hey," Brent said. "We never got autographs."

Gabe reached out and handed a card to each of us. They were yellow, and the words VAMPIRE NATION-GUEST were printed on each one in bold red letters.

"Wear that around your neck," Gabe instructed. "That will let everyone know that you have permission to be here. We've got about ten minutes before our next scene begins. Until then, you can wander around the stage. But when filming begins, you'll need to go up into the theater area."

We put looped the cords around our necks, and the cards dangled like gaudy necklaces. Gabe smiled. "Perfect," he said. "Miss Black says you're working on a school project?"

Michelle spoke. "That's right. I have a report

due tomorrow. It's about how television shows are made."

"You're lucky," Gabe said. "This is the final taping of the season. Most of the show is already complete, and there are only a couple scenes being filmed tonight." He looked around the stage and motioned to some of the crew members. "I think you could talk to some of the crew if you have questions. They know more about television production than I do. Is there anything else I can do for you?"

"No," I said. "Thanks."

Without saying anything more, Gabe turned and walked off, leaving the three of us alone.

"Everybody sure looks busy," I said. "Let's walk around and see if we can find the production studio."

"You three children aren't going anywhere," a thick, familiar voice said.

We turned to face a man, standing a few feet away, looking at us. He had a shock of dense, silvery hair, and was wearing black pants, a black turtleneck sweater, and a black blazer. His eyes were battleship gray, numbingly cold, and they seemed to bore into us.

And I knew. Although I hadn't seen his face before, I knew we were staring at Lou Turndacca, the man who was planning to turn everyone in the country into vampires.

He opened his mouth to speak, repeating himself, and he continued glaring at us with those frigid, polar ice eyes.

"You three children aren't going anywhere . . . ."

14

". . . until you sign the guest registration form."

I hadn't noticed it, but Lou Turndacca was carrying a clipboard. He held it out, along with a shiny, silver pen. "If you're going to be anywhere except the viewing theater," he said, "you must sign the guest registration form. Friends of Miss Black?"

We nodded. "Yeah," Michelle said. "We go way back. Old pals."

Lou Turndacca smiled, and it made me cringe. "Old pals, eh?," he said. Then, he looked at me and paused. "You look frightened, my young friend," he said. His voice sounded concerned, grandfatherly.

"Um, I, uh . . . I'm just nervous, I guess," I managed to say.

"Nothing to be nervous about," he said. He handed the clipboard to Brent, who signed his name. Then, he handed it to me. I signed, and passed the clipboard to Michelle. After she'd signed, she handed it back to Lou Turndacca.

"Thank you," he said. "Enjoy yourselves, and remember: when production begins, you mustn't be in the filming area. Go upstairs to the viewing theater. Nowhere else."

"Okay," I said, and Brent and Michelle nodded.

Lou Turndacca smiled, bowed slightly, turned, and walked away. When he disappeared, I spoke.

"That's him!" I hissed. *"That's Lou Turndacca, the Executive Producer! He's the guy I heard on the phone! He was the one I heard!"*

"He even *looks* like a vampire," Michelle said. "And did you see his eyes? Creepy! He's probably a thousand years old, like most vampires."

"Well, if he's not in the production studio," I said, "that means it might be empty. Now's our chance. Let's go up the stairs and into the theater. There's a hallway that leads to the studio."

We strode across the stage, down a half dozen steps, and over to a long, dimly-lit flight of stairs. At the top was a door that opened into the viewing theater. A single light on the far side of the theater was the only illumination, and the large room was gloomy and quiet. I could make out the dark shadows of empty seats, and an aisle that led to the back of the theater. Beneath the balcony, on and around the stage, crews continued to prepare for the show's taping.

"This way," I said, and I started out, making my way slowly through the dark theater. Michelle and Brent followed.

"It's kind of spooky without anyone else around," Michelle said.

"Let's just hope there's no one in the studio," Brent said.

We reached the back of the theater, and the large, closed double doors. Quietly, I pushed one. It opened, and I was relieved. I was afraid it might be locked.

Pushing the door open farther, I poked my head through and looked into the hallway.

Empty.

"Nobody in sight," I said, and I pushed the door all the way open. The three of us tiptoed down the hall silently, like cats stalking a bird.

We reached the door to the production studio. It was closed. I pointed to the floor, to the thin, dark shadow beneath the door. *"It doesn't look like there's a light on inside,"* I whispered. *"I think it's empty."*

Brent grasped the doorknob. It turned, and he slowly pushed the door open. The three of us slipped inside. The door closed behind us, and we were immersed in darkness, except for the soft glow of a single computer screen on the desk.

"We'd better figure out what we're going to do, and fast," said Michelle.

"We'd better find a light, first," Brent said.

I swept my hand over the wall, found a switch, and flipped it up. Harsh, stale light bloomed.

"Wow," Brent breathed as he surveyed the studio. "There's a lot of equipment in here."

He was right. There were racks and racks, stacks and stacks of equipment. Most of it appeared to be turned off, but there were several pieces of equipment on a long table with multicolored, glowing lights, like tiny eyes. The large, flat screen computer monitor on the desk displayed the images of some software programs.

Brent walked to the table and pushed aside an expensive-looking black leather chair. He stared at the computer screen, frowning. Michelle and I approached and stood next to him.

"What is it?" Michelle asked.

Brent pointed to some changing numbers on the screen. "I'm not sure," he said. "But that task bar reads 'importing low-level sound waves.' And look . . . that graph says it's over fifty percent finished."

"But where are the sound waves coming from?" I asked.

"They might be stored in the same computer," Brent replied. "If that's the case, it might be transferring the sound file and embedding it in the television episode. Then again, the sound might be coming from something else, like a peripheral."

"What's a peripheral?" Michelle asked.

"Just another piece of equipment that's plugged into a computer," Brent explained. "For instance, a printer is a peripheral. Or an external hard drive. Things like that."

"Good thing you know so much about computers," Michelle said.

Brent dropped to his hands and knees and found the computer box, the brain of the machine. "Hey," he said. "There's something strange connected to the computer by a cable. A black box of some sort. That might be where the sound waves are coming from." He stood. "Okay, here's what we're going to do. Michelle, stay by the door and look down the hall. Try to stay out of sight. If anyone comes, let us know. Amber, you help me—"

Just then, we heard something.

A voice.

A deep voice, and I recognized it right away. It was the Executive Producer, and it sounded like he was speaking into a phone. He was coming to his studio!

"Hide, quick!" I hissed.

"Let's get out of here!" Michelle shot back.

"No time!" I replied. *"If we leave now, he'll see us for sure. Find a place to hide in here."*

Brent scrambled under the table and behind the computer box. He would be able to hide there, safe and out of sight, but the space wasn't big enough for another person.

"The other side of the desk!" Michelle whispered. *"We can hide behind that stack of equipment!"*

I quickly clicked the light switch off. In the glow of the computer monitor, Michelle and I flew around the table, hunkered to the floor, and scrabbled behind a large rack of electronics. We'd be safe—as long as the man stayed on the other side of the desk.

And we were just in time, too. We heard the door open, and Lou Turndacca's dark, throaty voice. The overhead lights winked on. As he sat in his chair,

I couldn't help but think about my brother, under the table at that very moment. Brent was only a couple of feet away from him!

"Almost," Lou Turndacca said into the phone. "The subliminal sound waves are being attached to the episode right now, and it's almost finished. The final scenes are being filmed tonight, and I'll add them to the episode. No one has suspected anything. For many people, the change has already begun."

There was a pause, and then Lou Turndacca spoke again. "Yes, even in the city, many people are feeling the effects, although they don't know it. Many people have been overcome with an urge to become a vampire by dressing like us. They think it's their own desire to do this, but they have no idea that it's because of the hidden sound waves in each episode of *Vampire Nation*. Once the final episode airs, everyone watching will become like us, only we will rule them. First, the country, and then the world!"

I shuddered. What he was planning was truly horrible for every human on the planet.

But for us, things were about to get worse.

At that very moment, my phone in my pocket rang, singing out a loud, shrill tone that pierced the studio. I tried to grab it, but it rang again. Then, when I finally did pull it from my pocket, I accidentally dropped it. It flipped through the air and clanged to the floor, landing hard enough to knock the battery loose. The ringing stopped as the phone clattered to the floor.

But that wasn't the worst part. The worst part was when Lou Turndacca stood and spoke.

"I know you're in here," he said. His heavily-accented voice boiled with anger. "Come out. *NOW!*"

15

There was no way out.

Michelle and I were hunched on the floor, hiding behind a rack of electronics. We frantically looked around the studio, searching for a door, a window, any escape route. There was nothing. The only way out was the door that led to the hallway . . . and Lou Turndacca stood between us and the exit, blocking our way.

"I know you're in here," he growled. "Come out, now."

I looked at Michelle. Her eyes were wide, her expression that of overwhelming fear and uncertainty.

Slowly, I stood. My phone lay on the floor at my feet, broken open. The thin, square battery lay next to it. I wished I could have used it to call for help, but it was too late. I'm sure Michelle had her phone, but now that we'd been caught, I doubted she would have the chance to call anyone.

Michelle stood. Both of us, trembling and panic-stricken, stared at Lou Turndacca. He, too, was now standing, his head slightly bent slightly forward, his eyes narrowed, burning into us. One hand still held his phone to his ear. He looked furious.

"And what have we here?" he snarled, slowly lowering his phone. "A couple of young snoops. Tell me, young ladies: what was it you were hoping to find in here?"

"You're never going to get away with it!" I suddenly blurted.

A terrible smile creased his lips. "Oh?" he mocked. "And just what is it that I'm not going to get away with?"

"Turning everyone into vampires!" I said. "We know all about it. We know about you and the sound waves you put in *Vampire Nation*."

"Ah, yes," Lou Turndacca said. "Those pesky sound waves. And just what, my young friend, are you going to do about it, hmm? How do you intend to stop me?"

Suddenly, I remembered that I'd put one of the garlic bulbs in my coat that morning, before I went to school. I reached into my pocket, pulled it out, and held it up for him to see, thrusting my fist into the air in a display of power and victory.

Seeing the garlic bulb in my hand, Lou Turndacca winced and took a sudden step back, raising his arms and recoiling at the sight of the garlic. "Enough of this silliness!" he hissed. "Put that away! Put it away!"

I shook my head. "No way," I said. Getting

braver, I took a step around the rack of electronics, closer to Lou Turndacca.

Suddenly, Brent popped up from beneath the table. Lou Turndacca looked at him with surprise and shock, as he hadn't known Brent had been hiding.

"Hey," Brent said, "look what I found." He held up a large black box made out of metal. A cable attached to it ran beneath the desk, connected to the computer.

Seeing this, Lou Turndacca's expression changed. His face became even whiter, and deep frown lines appeared on his forehead. His gray eyes were like drops of frozen liquid.

"You . . . leave . . . that . . . alone!" he spoke, hissing the words, spacing them slowly. *"Put that down!"*

"Why?" Brent said. "What would happen if I accidentally dropped it?"

Lou Turndacca made a sudden move toward Brent, but I took a step closer and caught his attention. I was still holding the garlic bulb in my hand, and the sight of it caused him to back against the wall.

"Just leave," Lou Turndacca said. "Just leave, and I'll forget this ever happened. I'm warning you: if you don't leave now, you're all doomed."

"Boy," Brent said, cradling the metal box in his hands. "This is kind of heavy. I hope I don't drop it. It might break."

Lou Turndacca suddenly made a lunge for Brent, snarling like a vicious animal.

"Oopsy," Brent said . . . and he dropped the metal box and leapt back. It crashed to the floor with a heavy thud and a brisk shattering sound, like broken glass and china.

Lou Turndacca suddenly stopped. He stared at the floor in dumbstruck horror.

"Bummer," Brent said. "Sorry about that."

"You!" Lou Turndacca snarled. He looked like a coiled snake, ready to strike, but the garlic kept him away. *"You don't know what you've done! You don't know what you've—"*

Suddenly, Lou Turndacca froze. His eyes bulged, and veins in his neck popped beneath his skin like cords. He shuddered and shook.

Brent took a nervous step back. "What's going on?" he asked.

As if I knew! I had no idea what was happening, but it quickly became apparent that Lou Turndacca was vanishing!

"You fools!" he hissed. *"You think you've stopped me?!?! Well, you haven't! I'll be back. I am ageless and timeless, and I will return!"*

It was incredible, but Lou Turndacca was disappearing flesh and bone decaying before our eyes. His entire body became an odd, milky white. His skin seemed to be turning to smoke, swirling into the air and vanishing.

"Wow," Michelle whispered from behind me.

In less than thirty seconds, it was all over. There was no trace of Lou Turndacca.

"What just happened?" I asked Brent.

My brother shrugged. "I don't know," he said. "That box was the sound generator. It was hooked to the computer, and I figured that if I smashed it, the thing would stop sending the sound waves to the computer and stop embedding the brain waves into the television episodes."

"But that guy vanished," Michelle said.

"That was a lot easier than pounding a stake through his chest," I said.

The three of us were now standing around the very spot where Lou Turndacca had stood just a moment before.

"That black box must have been giving off some sort of sound wave that gave him the power to exist," Brent said. "When I smashed it, he lost his source of power."

"Is that even possible?" I asked.

Brent shrugged. "I guess so," he said. "I don't have any other explanation."

"But what did he mean about being 'ageless and timeless?'" I asked. "And he said he was going to return. What was that about?"

We had no answers. For whatever reason, destroying the mysterious black box had not only stopped the sound waves from being embedded in the episode, but it had also destroyed Lou Turndacca . . . at least for the time being.

On our way home, we continued talking about what had happened. We had no answers—only more questions, the biggest of which was: did we stop Lou Turndacca from turning everyone in the country into vampires? Brent hadn't done anything to damage the computer—just the strange black box generating the sound waves.

At school the next day, I noticed something odd.

No one was dressed like a vampire. Nobody. Cooper Winneker had gone back to his normal self, wearing blue jeans and a football jersey. His skin had regained its healthy, normal color. Even Mrs. Chesapeake, the librarian, had abandoned her vampire look, and she dressed as she always had. Not a single person had pasty white skin.

Brittany Collins stopped me in the hall. Her hair was no longer dyed black, and the pink streak was gone. She looked like an average fifth grader.

"I want to apologize," she said. "I told you that I hadn't come to your window that night. It's funny, but all of a sudden I remember it. My memory is hazy, but maybe I really did come to your window. But I feel like it wasn't even me, like it was someone else."

"Don't worry," I said. "I've already forgotten about it."

In the newspaper the next morning, Lou Turndacca was on the front page. It was reported that he'd mysteriously vanished. No one knew where he was, and another producer was flying in from Hollywood to put the finishing touches on the final episode of *Vampire Nation*. I hoped it wasn't the guy Lou Turndacca had been speaking with on the phone.

The week passed, and I waited anxiously for the last show. I had no desire to see it, especially after everything that had happened. But I was nervous. I hoped that we'd succeeded, and that no one would turn into a full-fledged vampire after watching the final episode.

But what about those who'd already turned? I wondered. *I hope that, somehow, they turn back to their normal selves.*

The day after the show aired, I walked

cautiously to school, carrying a garlic bulb in my coat pocket. I saw no signs of anyone who looked like a vampire. At school, everyone seemed normal . . . except Michelle.

She caught up with me in the lunchroom, and she was frantic, breathless. She was carrying an old book, and the same red notebook that she always had with her.

"You're not going to believe this!" she said, taking a seat next to me. I was eating a sandwich, and I put it down.

"I'll believe just about anything, after last week," I replied.

"Well, you're *not* going to believe what I found," she said. "I checked out this book from the public library."

She opened up the old volume, called *Vampire Lore: Fact and Fiction*. The pages were yellowed, and the ink had faded. It smelled musty and aged, like old, rotten wood. She flipped through the book until she found a drawing of a large castle. Then, she placed it on the table in front of me.

"That's where Count Dracula lived, years ago," she said. "That's his castle in Transylvania."

I looked at the drawing of the castle. "So?" I said.

"So," Michelle continued, "he lived there a long time ago. But vampires are un-dead. They live forever. If he's not in his castle, where is he?"

I shrugged, and took a bite of my sandwich. "I don't know," I said.

"Look at this. Your brother was right about those sound waves in that black box. This book says that Count Dracula is able to survive through generations because he is able to use low level sound waves—sounds that normal humans can't hear—as a source of energy. Despite what everyone thinks, vampires don't live on blood alone, but low level sound waves, too. Think about it, Amber. He's been around a long time, and has learned a lot. He's figured out how to generate his own low level sound waves, and he's figured out a way to make them strong enough to turn ordinary humans into vampires."

I thought about the black box Brent had

smashed, and how Lou Turndacca had vanished.

"And look here." She flipped a page and pointed to a paragraph. "Here, it says Count Dracula has been able to escape detection because he moves around a lot and changes his name."

"So?" I repeated. "Are you saying that—"

"—Look," Michelle said, and she pulled a pencil from her pocket and wrote COUNT DRACULA on her notebook. Beneath it, she wrote LOU TURNDACCA.

I stared, puzzled.

"Don't you see?" Michelle said excitedly. "His name is an anagram. You know: taking the letters of a word or words to make something totally different. If you take every letter from the words Count Dracula, they spell Lou Turndacca. There's not a single letter left out!"

I stared at the two names in stunned, silent disbelief.

Count Dracula?

Lou Turndacca, Executive Producer of Vampire Nation, *was none other than the real Count Dracula!*

"That's incredible!" I said.

"I know," Michelle said. "But it must be him."

"Then, where did he go?" I asked. "When Brent smashed the black box that was generating the sound waves, what happened to him?"

Michelle shook her head. "I don't know," she said. "But I don't doubt him for a minute. He said he'll return, and you can bet that he will. He's probably been popping up all over the world for the past thousand years. Somewhere on earth, maybe here, maybe in another country, Count Dracula will be back."

"And he's going to try to do what he tried with the *Vampire Nation* television series," I said, my voice barely a whisper. "He wants to create an entire world of vampires."

Michelle nodded. "Whatever happened to him, wherever he is, he won't stop until he has his way."

ooo

There were a lot of questions that remained unanswered. Where did Lou Turndacca—Count

Dracula—go? Who was it that he'd been speaking with on the phone? How was he able to create the mysterious black box that generated the sound waves that gave him power? If he was able to do it once, he'd be able to do it again.

What if he succeeds?

Ever since all of this happened, I've tried my best to live a normal life. I go to school, play soccer, and hang out with my friends. I ride my bike, I do my homework. I've tried to push away thoughts of vampires, but it's hard when so many new books are being written about them, and so many movies and television shows continue to be made.

Still, I'm always looking over my shoulder, watching. Waiting. Wondering: *Where is he going to be next? Where will Count Dracula appear?*

Vampire Nation, the television series, is over. The season has ended, the famous stars have moved on to work on other projects in different states. But for me, Brent, and Michelle, our own personal episode lives on, forever burned into our memories, haunting us like a lonely wind on a cold winter night, following us like our own footprints in the sand.

I don't like to admit it, but my life has changed. I don't stay out past dark, and I always make sure I'm indoors when the sun sets. I'm suspicious of anyone who wears black. I get nervous easily, and I'm often anxious and fretful. When I see someone reading a vampire book at school or on a park bench, I wonder if maybe, just *maybe*—

Lastly: I never, ever go to bed without placing a few bulbs of garlic under my pillow, just to have it handy.

And if I were you, I'd do the same.

THE END

ABOUT THE AUTHOR

Johnathan Rand is the author of more than 65 books, with well over 4 million copies in print. Series include **AMERICAN CHILLERS, MICHIGAN CHILLERS, FREDDIE FERNORTNER, FEARLESS FIRST GRADER**, and **THE ADVENTURE CLUB.** He's also co-authored a novel for teens (with Christopher Knight) entitled **PANDEMIA**. When not traveling, Rand lives in northern Michigan with his wife and three dogs. He is also the only author in the world to have a store that sells only his works: **CHILLERMANIA!** is located in Indian River, Michigan. Johnathan Rand is not always at the store, but he has been known to drop by frequently. Find out more at:

www.americanchillers.com

Attack of the Monster Venus Melon!

Here's what readers from around the country are saying about Johnathan Rand's AMERICAN CHILLERS:

"I love your books! Everyone in my school races to get them at our library. Please keep writing!"

-Jonathon M., age 13, Ohio

"I am your biggest fan ever! I'm reading MISSISSIPPI MEGALODON and it's awesome."

-Emilio S., Illinois

"I just finished KENTUCKY KOMODO DRAGONS and it was the freakiest book EVER! You came to our school, and you were funny!"

-Ryan W., age 10, Michigan

"I just read OKLAHOMA OUTBREAK. It was really great! I can't wait to read more of your books!"

-Bryce H., age 8, Wisconsin

"My mom ordered American Chillers books on-line from your website, and they were autographed by you! Thanks!"

-Kayla T., age 11, Louisiana

"I love to read your books at night, in bed, under the covers with a flashlight! Your stories really creep me out!"

-Chloe F., age 8, California

"Man, how do you come up with your crazy ideas? I've read 15 American Chillers, and I don't know which one I like best. Johnathan Rand ROCKS!"

-James Y., age 10, Nebraska

“Ever since you came to my school, everyone has been addicted to your books! My teacher is reading one to us right now, and it’s great!”

-Mark F., age 11, Kentucky

“You need to put more pictures of your dogs on your website. I think they’re super cute.”

-Michelle H., age 12, Oregon

”I have read every one of your American Chillers and Michigan Chillers books. The best one was WICKED VELOCIRAPTORS OF WEST VIRGINIA. That book gave me nightmares!”

-Erik M., age 9, Florida

“How do you come up with so many cool ideas for your books? You write some really freaky stuff, and that’s good.”

-Heather G., age 8, Maryland

“I met you at your store, Chillermania, last year. Thanks for signing my books for me! It was the best part of our vacation!”

-David L., age 13, Illinois

”A couple of years ago, I was too young to read your books and they scared me. Now, I love them! I read them every day!”

-Alex P., age 8, Minnesota

“I love your books, and I love to write. My dream is to come to AUTHOR QUEST when I’m old enough. My mom says I can, if I get accepted. I hope I can be a great writer, just like you!”

-Cynthia W., age 8, South Dakota

"Everyone loved it when you came to our school and did an assembly. You were really funny, and we learned a lot about writing and reading."

-Chad R., age 10, Arizona

"You are my favorite author in the whole world! I love every single one of your books!"

-Amy P., age 9, Michigan

"I heard that you wear those weird glasses when you write your books. Is that true? If it is, keep wearing them. Your books are cool!"

-Griffin W., age 12, Maine

"HAUNTING IN NEW HAMPSHIRE is the best ghost story ever! EVER!"

-Kaylee J., age 11, Tennessee

"I don't think anyone else in the world could write as good as you! My favorite book is NEBRASKA NIGHTCRAWLERS. Britney is just like me."

-Taylor, M., age 10, Michigan

"I used to hate to read, and now I love it, because of your books. They're really cool! When I read, I pretend that I'm the main character, and I always get freaked out."

-Jack C., age 9, Colorado

Got something cool to say about Johnathan Rand's books? Let us know, and we might publish it right here! Send your short blurb to:

Chiller Blurbs
281 Cool Blurbs Ave.
Topinabee, MI 49791

Other books by Johnathan Rand:

Michigan Chillers:

#1: Mayhem on Mackinac Island
#2: Terror Stalks Traverse City
#3: Poltergeists of Petoskey
#4: Aliens Attack Alpena
#5: Gargoyles of Gaylord
#6: Strange Spirits of St. Ignace
#7: Kreepy Klowns of Kalamazoo
#8: Dinosaurs Destroy Detroit
#9: Sinister Spiders of Saginaw
#10: Mackinaw City Mummies
#11: Great Lakes Ghost Ship
#12: AuSable Alligators
#13: Gruesome Ghouls of Grand Rapids
#14: Bionic Bats of Bay City

American Chillers:

#1: The Michigan Mega-Monsters
#2: Ogres of Ohio
#3: Florida Fog Phantoms
#4: New York Ninjas
#5: Terrible Tractors of Texas
#6: Invisible Iguanas of Illinois
#7: Wisconsin Werewolves
#8: Minnesota Mall Mannequins
#9: Iron Insects Invade Indiana
#10: Missouri Madhouse
#11: Poisonous Pythons Paralyze Pennsylvania
#12: Dangerous Dolls of Delaware
#13: Virtual Vampires of Vermont
#14: Creepy Condors of California
#15: Nebraska Nightcrawlers
#16: Alien Androids Assault Arizona
#17: South Carolina Sea Creatures
#18: Washington Wax Museum
#19: North Dakota Night Dragons
#20: Mutant Mammoths of Montana
#21: Terrifying Toys of Tennessee
#22: Nuclear Jellyfish of New Jersey
#23: Wicked Velociraptors of West Virginia
#24: Haunting in New Hampshire
#25: Mississippi Megalodon
#26: Oklahoma Outbreak
#27: Kentucky Komodo Dragons
#28: Curse of the Connecticut Coyotes

Freddie Fernortner, Fearless First Grader:

#1: The Fantastic Flying Bicycle
#2: The Super-Scary Night Thingy
#3: A Haunting We Will Go
#4: Freddie's Dog Walking Service
#5: The Big Box Fort
#6: Mr. Chewy's Big Adventure
#7: The Magical Wading Pool
#8: Chipper's Crazy Carnival
#9: Attack of the Dust Bunnies from Outer Space!
#10: The Pond Monster

Adventure Club series:

#1: Ghost in the Graveyard
#2: Ghost in the Grand
#3: The Haunted Schoolhouse

For Teens:

PANDEMIA: A novel of the bird flu and the end of the world
(written with Christopher Knight)

AMERICAN CHILLERS

AMERICA'S #1 SERIES FOR MAXIMUM CHILLS!

DOUBLE THRILLERS!

Vampire Nation & Attack of the Monster Venus Melon!

Johnathan Rand

An AudioCraft Publishing, Inc. book

Book storage and warehouses provided by Chillermania!©
Indian River, Michigan

Warehouse security provided by:
Lily Munster, Scooby-Boo, & Spooky Dude

American Chillers Double Thrillers:
Vampire Nation & Attack of the Monster Venus Melon!
ISBN 13-digit: 978-1-893699-26-7

Librarians/Media Specialists:
PCIP/MARC records available **free of charge** at
www.americanchillers.com

Cover illustration by Dwayne Harris
Cover layout and design by Sue Harring

Printed in USA

Dickinson Press Inc., Grand Rapids, MI USA Job # 3712100 April 2010

Attack of the Monster Venus Melon!

"Anthony! Hey, Anthony! Wait up!"

When I heard my name, I turned, squinting in the harsh sunlight. It was June 6th, the last day of school, and I was walking home. I was officially a sixth-grader.

Well, I would be a sixth-grader in three months, after the summer break. But that seemed like a lifetime away.

Three whole months, I thought. Swimming, riding my bike, fishing in the river, playing soccer, and hanging out with my friends. Three months of fun. Summer's promise drifted through my mind like a

dream.

In the distance, I saw Kiera Collins, my good friend and neighbor. She was riding her bike toward me, pedaling madly along the sidewalk, trying to catch up. I had been walking, and I stopped and waited for her.

"Summer vacation is finally here!" she panted as her bike rolled to a stop in front of me. "Isn't it great?"

"It sure is!" I agreed. "We're going to have a blast!"

"Anything yet?"

I knew exactly what Kiera was talking about. She and I had entered a science fair, sponsored by a local college. Teams of elementary school kids could enter for free. Over the summer, they needed to create some sort of science project and document the progress in a notebook. In September, everyone who entered would display their project at the college campus. The winning team, chosen by college professors, would share a one thousand dollar scholarship. That meant that if Kiera and I won, we would each have five hundred dollars to use for college in the future! I planned on going to college to become a doctor, so I was going to need all the money I could

get. Five hundred dollars would really be great . . . if we won.

If.

Our project was complex. We were going to try to blend two different plants together to create an all new species. We thought of crossing a tomato plant with a radish plant, or a carrot with an onion, but those seemed kind of boring. It was Kiera who came up with the perfect experiment. She suggested we try crossing a watermelon plant with a Venus flytrap, which is a small, insectivorous plant. An insectivorous plant is a type of carnivorous plant that catches and eats insects and spiders. The plant doesn't chew its food, but, rather, traps it in a pod where it is digested. We had one at school for a while. It was exciting to watch the plant eat a real, live insect. Problem was, too many kids overfed the plant by giving it too many bugs, and it died.

We had taped together one seed from each plant, put them in two small paper cups full of soil, and checked them every day. I know it doesn't seem very scientific, but we did a lot of research on growing watermelons and Venus flytraps. Growing watermelons, we learned, was easy. Venus flytraps, on

the other hand, required a little more care. Still, the idea of blending the two plants together seemed cool. If we could do it successfully, I knew we'd have a super cool plant . . . and a good chance at the scholarship money.

So far, however, we hadn't had much luck. Two weeks had gone by, and our plants still hadn't sprouted. I kept the cups on the windowsill in my bedroom and anxiously checked them each morning, but every day, I wrote a two-word notation in our progress journal.

Nothing yet.

I raised my hand to shield my eyes from the sun and looked at Kiera. Her wavy blonde hair gleamed, and her face had a thin sheen of perspiration. "Still nothing," I said, shaking my head. "At least, nothing had sprouted when I checked this morning before I went to school."

"I was hoping they would have started to grow by now," she said.

"Me, too," I replied. "If we could get them to grow, I'm sure we would win the scholarship."

"Oh, well," Kiera replied with a shrug. "At least we're trying. Do you want to go to the park later?"

I nodded. In the summer, a lot of neighborhood kids go to the park to play soccer. It's a lot of fun. "Yeah, that would be great," I said. "I'll meet you there after dinner."

"See you later," Kiera said, and she pedaled her bike around me and continued down the block. Usually, I ride my bike to school, too . . . but I'd broken the chain the day before and hadn't gotten it fixed. But I only lived six blocks from school, so it wasn't very far to walk.

When I got home, Trike was sitting on our front porch, waiting for me, just like he does every day. Trike is our dog—a yellow Labrador and pit bull mix—that we adopted from the animal shelter. Before we got him, he was injured by a car, and now he has only three legs. When we saw him at the shelter, he was so sweet and lonely that I just knew he was the perfect dog for our family, and it didn't matter if he had just three legs. Trike got around well, and not only is he a good dog, he's a great friend.

Trike let out a bark and wagged his tail.

"Hey, buddy!" I called out from the sidewalk. I slapped my leg with my hand. "Come and see me!"

Trike bounded off the porch and ran across the

lawn. For a dog that was missing his right front leg, he could run pretty fast.

I knelt to the grass and wrapped my arms around my dog. He licked my face and wagged his tail back and forth. “How’s it going, Trike?” I said as I scratched behind his ears. He responded by pressing against me, licking my ears, and nearly knocking me over.

I stood and walked across the lawn to the front porch. Trike followed at my heels, and as I opened the front door, he darted past me and went inside. I followed.

“I’m home, Mom!” I called out. Usually, Mom was still at work when I got home, but today was her day off.

“I’m upstairs, Anthony,” Mom replied loudly. “I’ll be down in a minute.”

I dropped my backpack on the couch and walked to my bedroom. Trike trotted into the kitchen and lapped up some water from his bowl.

The two paper cups—our science project—sat on the windowsill.

I stared.

Trike came into my room and nudged my leg,

but I hardly noticed him. I was too focused on the cups—or what was in the cups—to pay attention to my dog.

It's impossible! I thought. It just can't be possible!

Our plants had sprouted! Not only that, they were nearly six inches tall! They had sprouted and grown six inches since that very morning! They looked like little green fountains, rising from the paper cups.

I hurried to the window for a closer look. The shoots had thick stems, with a few long, bright green leaves. There was also an odd-looking green bulb on each plant, about the size of a golf ball. They didn't really look like watermelon plants, but they didn't look like Venus flytraps, either.

We did it! I thought. We created an entirely new species of plant!

I couldn't wait to tell Kiera. We'd all but given up on the project, thinking that it would be a failure. But the seeds had sprouted! The plants were growing, and fast.

Our science project progress journal was on my dresser, and I quickly began jotting down notes. I measured the plants and wrote down how tall each

one was. I was fascinated. It truly was amazing to see the young plants growing in the cups . . . but never in a million years could I have predicted that our science experiment would turn into something so deadly.

2

After I'd inspected the plants and made a few notes, I turned, raced into the kitchen, and picked up the phone. I poked at the numbers, and Kiera answered on the third ring.

"You're not going to believe this," I began, "but our plants have sprouted! They're actually growing!"

"What?!?!" she exclaimed.

"It's true," I said. "Each plant is already six inches tall. They've grown six inches since this morning!"

"That's impossible!" Kiera said. "I'll be right over!"

Five minutes later, Kiera and I were in my bedroom, staring in wonder at the plants on the windowsill.

"I still can't believe it," she said, shaking her head. "I've never heard of plants growing that fast."

"Well, it's an entirely new species of plant," I said. "It's bound to be different. We're going to win that scholarship, for sure!"

"I'd almost given up," said Kiera. "I didn't think they would ever grow."

"Me, too," I replied.

"What are we going to call them?" Kiera asked.

"How about 'Venus melons?'" I replied.

"How about 'Anthony and Kiera's super Venus melons?'" she suggested.

"Perfect!" I said. "We'll be famous! In September, everyone will know about Anthony and Kiera's super Venus melon plants!"

Trike came into the room carrying his stuffed hedgehog. It's his favorite toy in the world, and he loves to play fetch with it.

"Not now, buddy," I said, patting his head. "In a little while." Trike jumped onto my bed and laid down, still holding the stuffed toy in his mouth.

My mom appeared in the doorway.

"Hey, Mom!" I said. "Check this out." I pointed to the green shoots sprouting from the cups on the window sill. "Our plants are growing!"

Mom walked to where we were standing. She leaned over and looked curiously at the small plants.

"Very good," she said as she leaned closer. "That's impressive. I didn't think you'd be able to do it."

"We're going to call them 'Anthony and Kiera's super Venus melons,'" Kiera said. "We're going to be famous."

"And we're going to win that scholarship money," I added.

Over the next week, the plants continued to grow. In fact, they grew so rapidly that we had to replant them in plastic buckets. In seven days, they had grown to nearly two feet tall, and the bulbs had grown to the size of softballs.

Then one day, one of the plants died.

It was an accident, of course. Kiera and I were in my room, measuring the plants. I was detailing their progress in our journal. Kiera was drinking a bottle of Whippy Fizz soda pop, and she accidentally dropped it,

spilling the caramel-colored liquid all over the plant and into the soil.

"Bummer," she said as she picked up the bottle. "Sorry about that."

Neither one of us thought too much of it, but within a few minutes, the plant began to turn brown. A few minutes later, it had completely withered and died.

Kiera felt terrible. "I'm so sorry," she said. "I didn't think pop would hurt the plant."

"It's okay," I replied. "We still have one plant left. We'll just have to be careful, that's all."

Still, I had no idea of the trouble that was brewing. After all: who would think that a plant could be dangerous?

Then, late one night, I made a discovery that caused me to think seriously about our science project, and whether we were doing the right thing.

I had gone to bed after watching a movie. Trike was sleeping on the floor at the foot of my bed, just like he always does. Very rarely does he get up during the night, except to drink some water from his bowl in the kitchen. Sometimes, if we have a bad thunderstorm, he'll jump onto my bed because the

loud rumbles and crashing scare him. Mom doesn't want Trike on the bed, because she says he gets hair all over the place. Once in a while I sneak him up. But usually he sleeps on the floor, and he never moves or makes a sound during the night.

This particular night, however, I was awakened . . . by growling. Trike doesn't growl very often, and I was surprised.

I rubbed my eyes and tried to see in the murky gloom. I don't have a night-light in my bedroom, and my window blind was drawn to keep the streetlight from shining in.

"What's up, Trike?" I whispered groggily. I couldn't see him, but I could hear him in the darkness, at the foot of my bed, growling viciously. Something was bothering him, that was for sure, because he ignored me and continued to growl.

"Okay, okay, hang on," I said quietly.

I turned on the light next to my bed. Trike stood on his three legs, staring at the corner of my bedroom. His teeth were bared, and he looked like the most ferocious dog I had ever seen.

But when I saw what he was growling at, I completely freaked out.

3

The plant.

It was in the corner of my bedroom, where I'd placed it before I went to bed. During the day, I put it by the window to get sunlight, but I moved it across the room at night. When I'd placed it in the corner before going to bed, the plant was just over two feet tall.

Now, however, the plant had nearly doubled in size! It was as tall as I was, and the leaves had spread long and wide, giving it a fuller, bushy look.

I couldn't believe what I was seeing and, for a moment, wondered if I was dreaming. I rubbed my

eyes and squinted. The plant was still there, still the same size. I was awake, and I wasn't dreaming.

Trike continued to growl, and the hair on his back stood up.

"Trike, shh," I whispered. Trike stopped growling for a moment and looked at me. Then, he looked at the enormous plant and began growling again.

I pulled the covers back, swung my feet to the floor, and stood. Again, Trike looked at me, but he continued growling. For whatever reason, he felt threatened or scared by the plant.

I was amazed the Venus melon had grown so quickly in such a short time. Over the past week, it had continued to grow several inches a day, which was pretty fast.

But whoever heard of a plant doubling in size overnight? I wondered.

I tiptoed across the floor toward the plant. Trike held his ground and growled a little louder.

"Trike, that's enough," I said quietly. "It's just a plant."

Indeed, the plant was as tall as I was. The leaves were as wide as my hand and as long as my arm, and

they hung limply. The plant had truly doubled in size since I had gone to bed.

I reached out and gently touched one of the leaves. It was soft and smooth. I ran my finger along the stem, following it down to the bucket that we'd used as a planter. Now that the plant was so large, we'd have to replant it again, outside, as it had outgrown the bucket. Besides, if it kept growing as fast as it was, soon it would be touching the ceiling!

At the foot of my bed, Trike sat down. He continued his low growl.

"Oh, relax, Trike," I scolded gently. "It's a plant, not a burglar. It can't hurt you."

I turned, walked across my bedroom, climbed into bed, and clicked off the light.

Still, Trike continued to growl.

"Oh, all right," I whispered. "Get up here. Come on, bud." I patted the bed, and Trike got to his feet and leapt up.

Trike made a couple of circles before plopping down between my feet, curling into a ball. He was no longer growling.

I closed my eyes and thought about the plant. For sure, our experiment was a huge success. We'd

actually crossed two very different types of plants, and I was certain that we would win top prize at the science fair. That, of course, meant that Kiera and I would split the one thousand dollar scholarship. I fell asleep dreaming about plants, science fairs, and scholarships.

I didn't sleep long.

I was awakened by two things: Trike's low, rumbling growl . . . and a noise on the other side of my bedroom. I turned on the light.

Trike was still on the bed, laying down. His head was raised, and, once again, he was staring at the plant on the other side of the room.

I looked at the plant.

No, I thought. It's not possible.

I know it sounds crazy, but the plant seemed even bigger.

There's no way, I thought. It can't grow that fast.

Then, I noticed the bulb growing on the plant. It had been the size of a softball, but now it was even bigger. Not only that, it had a single, mouth-like slice going all the way around it, like it was splitting open.

I was fascinated and curious. I hadn't known

what to expect when the plant started to grow, and I wasn't sure what the plant would look like: a Venus flytrap or a watermelon. A little bit of both, I had thought. Still, I never imagined it would grow so fast.

Once again, I pulled the covers back, crawled out of bed, and crept across the floor. Trike remained on my bed, growling softly.

Before me, the plant stood motionless in the corner. Sure enough, it was taller. It had grown since the last time I'd awakened. I inspected the bulb, looking carefully at the single crease that went across it, and I wondered if, perhaps, the bulb would open, like the mouth of the Venus flytrap.

Now, remember: at the time, I had no reason to be afraid. After all, it was just a plant. I was more amazed than anything, and I certainly wasn't afraid, even if the plant was scaring my dog.

I reached out and touched the bulb with my index finger. It was solid and hard. I leaned closer for a better look and ran my finger along the crease on the bulb.

Without warning, the crease opened. The bulb came alive, rearing back on its stem, opening even more. I tried to pull my hand away, but it was too

late. The bulb struck like a viper, clamping down on my hand!

4

I struggled to get the plant to release my hand, but it wouldn't! My hand didn't hurt, but I couldn't believe that the plant was so strong. It wouldn't let go!

Trike bounded off the bed and ran to the plant, barking and growling. He had known all along that something was wrong, but I hadn't listened to him.

Finally, after much pulling and wiggling, I was able to yank my hand free from the bulb. I wasn't hurt, no blood had been drawn, and there wasn't a single scratch on my hand. As soon as I'd pulled it out, the bulb snapped shut. The plant was still.

This is totally crazy, I thought. I was attacked by

my very own plant!

Trike had stopped barking and growling, but his loud ruckus had been enough to wake my parents. My dad appeared at my bedroom door, wearing his blue pajamas. His hair was all messed up, and he was squinting.

"What's all the racket about, Anthony?" he asked.

"My plant attacked me!" I said, holding up my hand. "The thing tried to eat my hand!"

Dad looked at the plant, then at me. He rolled his eyes. "You were having a nightmare," he said. "Go back to bed, and tell Trike to do the same. We all need to get some sleep." Then, he turned and walked down the hall.

"I should have figured that he wouldn't believe me, Trike," I said. "Come on. Let's hit the sack. You can sleep on my bed if you want, but make sure Mom doesn't find out."

I crawled back into bed, and Trike jumped up and curled at my feet.

And I must admit I was a little nervous: after all, the Venus melon had attacked me. It had clamped onto my hand and wasn't going to let go. Still, I never

thought of it as vicious or even dangerous. It was a plant, and nothing more. Soon, I fell back to sleep.

When I awoke in the morning, the plant hadn't changed much. Oh, it was still as big as ever, but it didn't appear to have grown over the past few hours. I crawled out of bed to inspect it closer. It seemed unchanged. The bulb was the same size, and its mouth was closed.

Wait until Kiera finds out about this, I thought as I changed out of my pajamas and into a pair of shorts and a T-shirt. *She's going to flip out.*

"Come on, Trike," I said. "You need to go outside." Trike barked once and followed me down the hall and into the kitchen, where Dad was making breakfast. I opened the back door and let Trike out. We have a big yard, with a huge maple tree in the middle. It's great for climbing. Mom has a flower garden at the back of the yard, and although we don't have a fence, tall shrubs grow at the edges of our property. Trike stays in the yard, and I don't have to put him on a chain.

"Have any more nightmares?" Dad asked as I closed the back door.

"It wasn't a nightmare," I said, shaking my

head. "It really happened. The plant grabbed my hand."

"Pretty soon, it'll be gobbling up the neighborhood," Dad said with a laugh. "I think I saw an old movie about that once, about a plant that went crazy and attacked people. Maybe you shouldn't be doing this experiment. Someone might get hurt." He was smiling, and I knew that he was joking.

"Wait until we win the scholarship," I said smartly. "You'll see."

After breakfast, Trike and I went across the street to Kiera's house.

"Wait until I tell you what happened last night!" I told her. We were standing in her garage, and she was cleaning her bike. We'd talked about going for a bike ride that day, being that I'd finally fixed my broken chain. Trike was busy sniffing around the yard.

"What happened?" she asked. "Did the plant grow some more?"

"Yeah," I replied. "Like you wouldn't believe. It doubled in size, and the bulb opened and grabbed my hand! It wouldn't let go!"

Kiera stopped cleaning her bike and stared at me. "What?!?!" she exclaimed.

I nodded my head. “Just like a Venus flytrap,” I said. “Only the bulb doesn’t look like the mouth of a Venus flytrap. Actually, it’s starting to look more like a head.”

“‘I’ve got to see it!” Kiera said. “The bike ride can wait!”

We rushed across the street to my house, with Trike at our heels.

“Did it hurt you?” Kiera asked as we raced up the front porch.

“Nah,” I said, opening the front door. “It just surprised me. It sure held on tight, though. I had a hard time getting my hand away from it.”

When we got to my bedroom, Kiera was shocked to see the size of the plant.

“You’re right!” she exclaimed with a gasp. “The thing doubled its size overnight!” She reached out and touched one of the leaves with her hand.

“Careful,” I said. “Don’t get too close to the bulb.”

Kiera quickly drew her hand back. “Maybe this isn’t such a good idea,” she said. “Maybe we shouldn’t be doing this experiment.”

“It’s just a plant, Kiera,” I replied. “Besides . . .

it's probably not going to get much bigger."

"I don't know," Kiera said warily. "What if it had hurt you?"

"Well," I replied, "that would have been different. But it didn't hurt me. We just have to remember to keep our hands away. Everything will be fine. Our plant is going to be famous! Not only that, we're going to win the science fair and the scholarship money."

And that was that. I made a few more notes in our progress journal, and Kiera and I went for our bike ride. Then, we went to the park. I came home for lunch, and we spent the rest of the afternoon in Kiera's backyard. Her family has an above-ground swimming pool, so we swam and played in the water all day. Trike hung out with us, chasing chipmunks in Kiera's backyard. Because he had only three legs, he was nowhere near fast enough to catch the small creatures. But he sure tried hard.

"Well, I'd better head home," I said. It was late afternoon. Mom and Dad would be home from work soon, and it would be time for dinner.

"Call me in the morning and let me know how our Venus melon is doing," Kiera said as she climbed

out of the pool. She picked up her beach towel and draped it around her shoulders.

"I will," I said. "I hope it doesn't get much bigger. In fact, let's plan on replanting it tomorrow. It's too big to keep in the bucket. Let's plant it in our backyard, where it will have more room to grow."

"Okay," Kiera said. "Just give me a call, and I'll come over and help."

We said our good-byes, and Trike and I walked across the street to my house. Both cars were gone, so I knew instantly that Mom and Dad were still at work.

Cool, I thought. *I'll have a chance to get cleaned up before dinner, and I can play my music loud without Mom or Dad yelling at me.*

I walked into our house, not knowing the horror that was waiting for me in my very own bedroom.

5

At first, I didn't notice anything unusual.

I walked into my bedroom, and the first thing I did was glance over at the plant in the corner. It hadn't grown, hadn't changed any since I'd been gone.

Or . . . had it?

There was something different about it, but I wasn't sure what it was. I stepped closer.

The leaves were the same size, and the Venus melon didn't appear to be any taller. But the bulb! It had opened up! Not only that, it had two rows of what appeared to be teeth. In fact, the bulb looked a lot like the pod on a Venus flytrap, only much bigger.

"Wow," I said, inspecting the plant further. But I remembered what had happened the night before, and I was careful not to get too close. The bulb appeared to be more and more like a small head. Of course, it didn't have ears or eyes or a nose, but now that it was open, showing rows of what appeared to be teeth, it looked—

Alive? Is that the right word?

Of course it was alive. It was a plant. But now the Venus melon seemed to have a different characteristic, like it was changing from plant to animal. It was a little scary, but it was also fascinating. Here we were, two kids not even in sixth grade, and we'd created an entirely new species of plant.

A Venus melon.

Trike came into my bedroom and immediately started growling at the plant. I patted his head. "It's okay, Trike," I said. "It's just a plant. It can't hurt you." Still, Trike continued to growl. He certainly didn't like the Venus melon, and he stayed away from it.

I made some notations in our progress journal, detailing the most recent changes, noting the change in the bulb and the teeth. The plant was looking more and more like a Venus flytrap, although the stems and

leaves were becoming long and twisted, vine-like, similar to a watermelon plant.

I turned on the radio in my bedroom and cranked up the volume. Mom and Dad don't like loud music, but if they're not home, they don't care. Just as long as it doesn't disturb the neighbors. Then, I changed into a pair of shorts and a tank top. All the while, Trike sat on a rug in my bedroom. He was no longer growling, but he watched the plant with a keen suspicion.

In looking at the plant again, I became wary. I wasn't scared, I wasn't afraid of the plant, but I was a little nervous. I wasn't sure if I wanted the plant in my room any longer. It was getting big, and maybe it should be outside . . . where it couldn't grab my hand again. I remembered what had happened the night before, how the bulb had lunged at me with the speed of a rattlesnake, snaring my hand. I didn't want that to happen again.

I decided not to wait until the following day to replant the Venus melon. I put on my sneakers and picked up the bucket that contained the plant. It was heavy, but I managed to carry it out of my bedroom, through the kitchen, and out the back door. Trike

followed a few steps behind, watching the plant like a prison guard.

I placed the Venus melon on the patio next to a lawn chair and paused. The air smelled of freshly-mowed grass, flowers, and barbecue. Next door, I could hear some younger kids playing. The sun was still high, but it was behind the trees. A few white clouds, like islands, hung in the blue sky.

Where should I plant the thing? I wondered as I gazed around the yard. I figured the best place would be near the back, a few feet from Mom's flower garden.

I picked up the bucket and carried the plant into the backyard. Next door, several kids laughed, and I caught a glimpse of movement through the bushes. They were playing catch with a ball, and they were having a great time. A blue jay landed in the big maple tree in the middle of the yard and squawked at me once before flying off. Far away, I heard a car horn honk.

I found a good place for replanting that was a few feet from Mom's garden. I knew that my parents would get mad if I dug a hole in the lawn, so I found a spot where no grass grew.

Now, to dig a hole, I thought.

I left the plant and walked to the garage, where I found a shovel. Then, I returned to the back of the yard and began digging a hole. All the while, Trike sat on the patio, watching me.

In the yard next door, the kids continued playing. They were throwing the ball wildly into the air, but it didn't sound like they were doing a very good job of catching it. Still, they were having fun.

I finished digging the hole and dropped the shovel. Now came the tricky part: getting the Venus melon out of the bucket. If I wasn't careful, I could damage the roots, which could injure or even kill the plant. Then, all of our work would be for nothing.

A movement in the sky caught my attention, and I looked up. One of the kids had made a wild throw, and a blue plastic ball was coming down in our yard. Right toward me, in fact.

I reached up to catch the ball . . . but the plant beat me to it! The stem sprang, and the bulb shot up, its teeth-filled mouth gaping wide, snatching the blue ball out of the air! It closed its mouth around it, and the ball vanished. Then, the plant was motionless once again, like nothing had happened.

It was incredible, but it was also horrifying.

It really is becoming more like an animal than a plant, I thought. The thing seems to have a mind all its own.

And now, the thing had eaten the neighbor kids' ball? How was I going to tell them that it had been eaten by a plant?

It was a problem, all right . . . but it was nothing like the trouble that was coming.

6

Within seconds of the Venus melon snapping the ball from the air, I was swarmed with little kids, most of whom I recognized from around the neighborhood. They had slipped through the bushes, looking for their ball.

One of the kids, wearing jeans and a red shirt, spoke. “Have you seen my ball?” he asked.

I shook my head. “No,” I said, “I haven’t.” I knew it was a lie, and I felt bad. But I couldn’t tell them that it had been eaten by the plant. Things like that would give little kids nightmares. I didn’t want any of them going to bed thinking that a vicious plant

might sneak into their bedroom and bite their arm . . . or worse.

A half dozen kids swarmed around me, looking for the blue ball.

"I'm sure it came this way," one of the kids said.

"You're welcome to look around," I said. "But I don't see it."

The kids searched the yard. Trike scampered around, and some of the kids played with him and patted his head. Trike gets along well with everyone.

After a few minutes of scanning the yard, the kids left. I still felt bad about the plant eating their ball, and I felt bad about lying to them. I decided to go to the dollar store in the morning to see if I could find another one for them.

Mom and Dad came home. While we ate dinner, I told them about the Venus melon. Later, I took them into the backyard to see where I'd replanted it.

"How exciting," Mom said. "You've created an entirely new kind of plant."

"It looks like a very large Venus flytrap," Dad said as he inspected the plant. "Except the stems and leaves are longer, like vines."

"That's because watermelons grow on vines," I

said. "The plant has characteristics of both the Venus flytrap and a watermelon."

"Has it tried to bite you again?" Dad asked with a smirk. I knew that he hadn't believed me from the night before. "Maybe it'll bite my hand, too."

I couldn't believe it, but my dad reached out and held his hand right in front of the closed bulb!

"I wouldn't do that if I were you," I warned. "That thing is going to clamp onto your arm and not let go."

Then, Dad actually touched the bulb! He ran his hand across it before pulling it away. Nothing happened, and the plant didn't attack him.

Strange.

I slept better that night, knowing that the Venus melon wasn't in my bedroom. I wasn't really afraid of it, but it still made me a bit uneasy. It had clamped down on my hand pretty hard. Now, the bulb was even bigger, and it had what appeared to be teeth. The teeth probably weren't sharp, but that didn't matter. Just the thought of a plant that big attacking my arm was enough to give me the creeps.

The next morning, I overslept. By the time I got up, Mom and Dad had already gone to work. I let Trike

out the front door, and then I poured some cereal into a bowl. I was going to turn on the television, but, instead, I picked up the cereal bowl, walked to the kitchen window, and looked into the backyard. One of the little neighbor kids was poking around in the bushes, probably looking for the plastic ball, and I reminded myself to walk to the dollar store to see if I could buy another one. I still felt bad they'd lost it, and I felt bad that I'd lied to them . . . but I just couldn't tell them that it had been eaten by a plant.

The boy walked over to Mom's flower garden and began searching through the plants. Just then, I heard Trike paw at the front door. He gave one single bark: that was his signal that he wanted in.

I put my cereal bowl on the counter, walked to the front door, and opened it. Trike bounded inside with a funny three-step hop, wagging his tail like crazy. I went back into the kitchen, picked up my cereal bowl, and looked out the window.

A chill went down my spine.

The boy had stopped searching Mom's flower garden, and now he was only a few feet from the Venus melon. Not only that, I could see the bulb starting to open, exposing its long teeth.

The boy was looking the other way and wasn't paying any attention to the plant. I put down my cereal bowl so hard that milk and corn flakes spilled all over the counter. I was just about to throw open the back door and yell, when the worst possible thing happened.

The Venus melon attacked the little boy!

7

There was nothing I could do. There wasn't time for me to shout a warning, to run and help the boy, nothing. Like lightning, the plant struck out at the boy just like it had attacked me in my bedroom.

Fortunately for the little kid, he was far enough away, and the plant missed him by mere inches. The large bulb snapped its jaws closed as it lunged, but it hadn't been able to grab the kid.

And the boy didn't even know the Venus melon had tried to grab him! He was looking the other way, searching for his ball, and had no idea that the plant had attacked.

When I opened the door, I called out to him. "Hey," I said, stepping onto the patio. The boy looked up at me. "Did you find your ball?" I asked.

He shook his head and looked very sad. "No," he said. "It's gone. I looked everywhere."

"Well, it might turn up," I said. "I'll tell you what: you go home, and I'll search my yard. If I find your ball, I'll bring it to your house."

"Okay," the little kid said. He stuffed his hands in his pockets and walked away, sullen and disappointed. As soon as he was gone, I darted back inside.

"Come on, Trike," I said. "We're going to the dollar store."

Trike waited outside while I went into Dollar Daze, which is only a few blocks from our house. Thankfully, I found a blue plastic ball that looked just like the one the little kids had been playing with. And it was only ninety-nine cents! I bought the ball and carried it home. Trike followed behind me happily, wagging his tail.

When I got home, I saw some of the little kids playing in the backyard next to ours. I walked over to them, carrying the ball.

"Is this yours?" I asked.

The boys looked at me. "You found our ball!" one of them shouted happily. I tossed the ball to him, and he almost caught it. Instead, it fell to the grass, and all the kids scrambled after it.

That's one problem solved, I thought. But I have to keep them out of the yard and away from the plant.

"I'll tell you what," I said. "Try to keep the ball in your yard. My mom has a flower garden growing, and she doesn't like anyone to get near it."

"Okay," the little kids said, and they began tossing the ball to one another.

Now, on to more serious problems, I thought.

I looked at the Venus melon. The sun was shining, and the plant was bright green and glossy. The bulb's mouth was open wide, and I could see the upper and lower rows of long teeth.

As much as I don't want to, I thought, we have to get rid of the plant. It's too dangerous. We're going to lose the science fair and the scholarship money, but it's better than someone getting hurt by the plant.

I went inside and called Kiera, but I didn't explain anything to her on the phone. Instead, I asked her to come to my house and told her that it was really

important. She said she'd be right over.

"This thing is getting way out of hand," I told her. We were standing on the patio in our backyard, looking at the plant. "Last night, that thing ate a little kid's ball. This morning, it attacked a little boy."

Kiera's eyes widened. "Did he get hurt?" she asked.

I shook my head. "Luckily," I replied, "he was far enough away, and the plant missed him. He never even knew the Venus melon had attacked. But it's only a matter of time before someone gets hurt . . . or worse."

"I want to take a closer look at it," Kiera said. She stepped off the patio and walked across the grass to the back of the yard, stopping a few feet away from the plant. I followed her. Trike had been sitting on the patio, and he didn't move. He still didn't want anything to do with the plant.

"Keep your distance," I said. "That thing can lunge without warning."

"You know," Kiera said, "maybe it's hungry. Maybe if we fed it something, it might stop snapping at people."

"But what are we going to feed it?" I asked.

"Venus flytraps eat bugs, and there aren't any bugs big enough for that thing to eat."

"What do you have in your refrigerator?" Kiera asked.

I shrugged. "I don't know," I replied. "The usual stuff, I guess."

"Do you have any hamburgers or hot dogs?" asked Kiera. "How about a steak?"

"I don't think so," I said, shaking my head. "There might be some lunch meat and some cheese. Probably some vegetables."

"Let's go have a look. There's got to be something we can feed it."

We strode through the yard and into the house. Trike had found a spot to lay down, and he remained on the patio.

"Maybe we can make it a sandwich," I said as we surveyed the contents of the refrigerator. Suddenly, I remembered something, and I opened up the freezer door. A blast of cold air struck my face as I moved some of the frozen items around.

"What?" Kiera said. "What have you got?"

"I think there's a—yes!" I pulled out a box. "A frozen pizza! This will be perfect!"

"Do you think the plant will eat it if it's frozen?" Kiera asked.

"I'll nuke it for a couple of minutes to thaw it out," I said.

I opened the box and tore away the plastic wrapping, then placed the pizza in the microwave. I hated to do it, because it was a pepperoni and sausage pizza—my favorite. But there really wasn't anything else to feed the plant.

After two minutes, the pizza had thawed a little. It was still a little stiff, but that would make it easier to carry and throw. I pulled it out of the microwave and put it on a cookie sheet I'd pulled out of the cabinet.

"Let's see if our Venus melon will eat this thing," I said. I picked up the cookie sheet with the pizza, and Kiera followed me outside. On the patio, Trike caught a whiff of the pizza and raised his head. He sniffed the air and wagged his tail.

"No, this isn't for you, buddy," I said.

We approached the Venus melon cautiously. I didn't want to get too close—just close enough to toss the pizza to the plant.

For a moment, I thought about how silly all of this was. Here we were, in my backyard, preparing to

feed a pizza to a plant! It sounded crazy.

I grabbed the pizza with my right hand, like I was going to fling a flying disc.

"Supper time!" I said, and I flung the pizza in the air toward the plant.

What happened next was incredible. The Venus melon had been perfectly still, but when the pizza came at it, the bulb came alive. It was like a ravenous beast! Its mouth opened even wider, and it struck out on its stem. The bulb snatched the pizza out of the air in a split-second, then clamped down on it. The pizza was gone.

"Holy cow," I whispered. "We've created a monster."

And we had. In our backyard was a monster like the world had never known, a creation of our very own. We'd successfully crossed two different plants together to create an entirely new species: a Venus melon. It was an incredible creation, a scientific miracle.

Whether it was right or wrong, I didn't know. I mean . . . when we first thought about the idea of crossbreeding two plants, it seemed harmless.

Now, I wasn't so sure.

And one thing we were about to discover was that feeding the pizza to the plant was one of the worst things we could have possibly done . . . we just didn't know it yet.

8

It happened the very next morning.

I had been awakened early by a thunderstorm. The rain pounded the roof, and lightning flashed, illuminating my bedroom. Thunder snarled and boomed. Trike didn't like the loud noise and became frightened, so I let him get up on my bed. He curled up next to me, and we both went back to sleep.

I'm not sure when it stopped raining, but the next time I awoke, the sun was out. It was just past seven; Dad had already left for work and Mom was getting ready to leave.

"Good morning, sunshine," Mom piped happily

as I walked into the kitchen. “Would you like some scrambled eggs and toast?”

“Yeah,” I replied. “That sounds great.”

“Did the storm wake you last night?”

I nodded. “Yes. The thunder was loud.”

“It rained hard,” Mom said as she pulled the eggs from the refrigerator. “We needed it. It’s been too dry for too long.”

After breakfast, Mom left for work, and I watched television. I scanned through the channels until I found a documentary on the Amazon rain forest.

And that’s when I remembered our Venus melon. Oh, I hadn’t forgotten about it, by any means. But I hadn’t yet checked on it that morning.

I got up from the couch and went into my bedroom to retrieve my journal. Then, I strode through the kitchen and walked to the back door.

“Trike?” I called out. My dog was in the living room, sitting near the couch. His ears went up, and he looked at me, but he didn’t move.

“Wanna go outside?” I asked.

Trike didn’t move. He let out a low whimper, and that was all.

"What's the matter?" I asked. "You don't want to go outside?" Usually, Trike followed me everywhere I went. He sure was acting strangely.

"Suit yourself," I said, and I opened the back door and stepped out onto the patio.

The air was crisp and cool. It smelled clean and fresh, like it always does after a good, hard rain. There was a hint of flowers in the air, drifting from Mom's garden. The grass was shiny and wet, and it glowed in the morning sun. Birds chirped. These are all things I noticed . . . until I saw the Venus melon. Then, I forgot about everything else.

The plant—the Venus melon Kiera and I had created—had more than tripled its size overnight. It now stood at least ten feet tall, and its bulb was no longer a bulb. It, too, had grown. It was now the size of a garbage can, and its gaping, hungry mouth was open, filled with two rows of long, narrow teeth, each nearly a foot long. I could even see what appeared to be eyes, glaring back at me. The plant had taken on a menacing, sinister look, like some Hollywood monster.

That's what it is, I thought. It's a monster. We've really created a monster.

I was scared. Just how big was the thing going

to get?

It was then that I realized that feeding pizza to the plant hadn't been the right thing to do. The food, combined with the rain, had caused the Venus melon to grow to enormous proportions. The question was: just how big would the thing get? What would it eat? Animals? Humans?

It was a horrifying thought. I'd figured all along that Kiera and I would be famous for creating an all-new kind of plant, and we'd win the scholarship money, for sure. Never in a million years did I think we'd create the living beast that we had. We would be famous, all right, and I knew that if we didn't destroy the plant, if we didn't stop it from growing, we were going to be in a lot of trouble. We might even go to jail, especially if the plant hurt someone or destroyed something.

Frantic, I went back inside and called Kiera. Her mother answered the phone and said that Kiera was still sleeping.

"Can you wake her up, Mrs. Collins?" I pleaded. "It's an emergency."

"Is something wrong?" Mrs. Collins asked.

"No," I replied. "Not yet. Our science project is

just a little out of control, that's all."

"Hang on, and I'll go wake her up."

After waiting for nearly a minute, I heard Kiera's thin, sleepy voice.

"Hello?" she said groggily.

"Kiera," I said, "you've got to come over here. Right now. This very minute."

"Anthony, I'm still in my nightgown. And I haven't eaten breakfast."

"Change into some clothes. Breakfast can wait. Get over here as soon as you can."

"What's wrong?" she asked.

"Lots," I said. "I'll tell you when you get here."

I hung up. Now, there was no doubt in my mind that we had to destroy the plant. Our little experiment wasn't so little anymore. It was over ten feet tall . . . and dangerous. And while I'd already made up my mind that we would have to kill the plant and abandon our experiment, I had no way of knowing that the plant had a plan of its own.

9

Kiera arrived ten minutes later. Her hair had been hastily combed, and she still looked sleepy.

"What's going on?" she asked.

"Come here," I said, and she followed me through the house to the back door. I opened it, and we stepped out onto the patio.

When she saw the plant, she gasped. If she wasn't awake before, she certainly was now.

"How . . . how did that thing get that big?!?!" she asked.

"Probably the pizza and the rain," I said.

"It's gigantic!" Kiera said.

"I don't think we have any choice, now," I said. "We've got to destroy it before it gets bigger."

"But how?" Kiera asked. "I don't want to get anywhere near that thing."

"Neither do I," I said, shaking my head. "That thing could probably scoop us up and eat us alive. But I have an idea. Remember when the plants first started growing? When we had two plants?"

Kiera nodded. "Yeah," she answered.

"Remember how you accidentally spilled Whippy Fizz on the plant, and it died?"

Kiera's eyes lit up. "You don't think—"

"That's exactly what I think," I interrupted. "I think we can use Whippy Fizz to kill the plant."

"Do you think it will work?" she asked.

"It might," I said. "Just think of how fast it killed the plant when you spilled the Whippy Fizz on it."

Kiera grimaced. "You know," she said, "if the Whippy Fizz was that bad for the plant, just imagine what it probably does to our stomachs."

I hadn't thought about that. Whippy Fizz was just soda pop, but maybe it wasn't all that good for the human body . . . especially if it could be used as a powerful plant killer.

"Let's give it a try," I said. "We have some Whippy Fizz in the refrigerator."

I walked back inside, and Kiera followed. In the fridge, I found a two-liter bottle of Whippy Fizz. I poured some of it into an empty mayonnaise jar I found in the cupboard.

"Let's give it a try," I said.

"But Anthony," Kiera said, "are you going to pour it on the plant? What if it attacks you?"

I shook my head. "I'm not going to get that close," I replied. "Just close enough to throw the Whippy Fizz. Hopefully, enough of it will land on the plant and kill it."

I opened the back door, and we walked outside. Trike followed us to the patio . . . but that was as far as he went. He stood on his three legs, watching the plant at the back of the yard. The hair on the back of his head stood up, and he let out a couple of low, deep growls.

"Here goes," I said, stepping off the patio.

"Be careful," Kiera said. "Don't get too close."

I carefully carried the jar of Whippy Fizz across the lawn, and my eyes never left the plant at the back of the yard. Then, a word popped into my head.

Surreal.

It was a word we'd learned in school. It meant 'having a dreamlike quality, not real, odd or strange.' That's what this whole thing felt like. It all felt very surreal, like what was going on right now couldn't be real and shouldn't be happening. But it was. Everything going on around me—including the monster Venus melon—was real.

When I was about eight feet from the gigantic plant, I stopped. I turned to look back, but only for a moment. Kiera and Trike remained on the patio, watching me.

Unfortunately, that was all the time the plant needed. In a split-second, the giant mouth had lunged out. I didn't even have a chance to run, as the enormous mouth had already closed around my left leg, and I fell to the ground, screaming. The jar of Whippy Fizz tumbled harmlessly to the grass, where the dark liquid quickly soaked into the soil and vanished.

Trike began barking. Kiera was screaming. I was yelling and kicking like crazy, trying to get my foot out of the plant's mouth. However, its jaws were so powerful that there was no way I was going to be able

to pry myself away.

And wouldn't you know who came to my rescue? My old pal and best friend.

Trike.

He appeared in a flash, snapping and snarling, growling and barking, nipping at the plant. Leaves and branches lashed down at him, but Trike spun and easily avoided them. Even with three legs, Trike could still move quickly when he needed to. He zigged and he zagged, weaving around and about. Finally, he lunged forward and snapped at the Venus melon, taking a big chunk from its stalk.

The mouth that had ensnared my leg suddenly released its grip and let out a loud, shrill squeal! I'd never heard a plant make a noise before . . . but, then again, I'd never been attacked by a plant, either.

I didn't waste a single second, pulling my foot away and rolling back. My skin and clothing became dew-soaked, but I barely noticed it. I just wanted to get as far away from that plant as possible.

After I'd rolled seven or eight times, I stood and ran to the patio. I had been lucky . . . but unfortunately, Trike wasn't.

In one single lightning-fast movement, the

entire plant bent over. The giant, open mouth struck out, seizing Trike. My dog made a single, terrified yelp just as the mouth closed around him and rose back into the air.

Trike—my very best friend in the whole world—was gone.

10

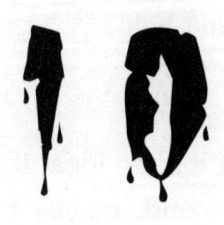

For the moment, all I could do was stare. I was horrified and shocked. Trike had saved my life, but, in doing so, he'd lost his. The plant had gobbled him up like he was a big, furry cupcake.

But it might not be too late. I'd read that Venus flytraps don't chew their food. Rather, they just trap their prey inside and secrete juices that slowly begin to dissolve it. If I acted fast, I might be able to save Trike.

But how?

I leapt off the patio and ran to the garage. I looked around to find something I could use as a weapon.

A rake?

No.

A shovel?

Nope. I'd have to get too close.

Lawn mower?

That wouldn't help.

Basketball?

Wait a minute.

Suddenly, I had an idea. If I could distract the plant for just a second, maybe I could trick it into opening its mouth. If that happened, Trike might be able to get out!

I picked up the basketball and dashed into the yard. The plant was motionless, as if nothing at all had happened. Kiera still stood on the patio, her face an expression of disbelief and horror.

I ran closer to the plant, being careful not to get too close.

"Hey, you big, green, leafy ogre! Eat this!"

And with that, I threw the basketball at the Venus melon, where it struck the giant, blub-like head, bounced off, and fell to the ground.

The plant sprang to life, bending over. The enormous head opened its mouth to attack the

basketball . . . and Trike leapt out! He tumbled once when he lost his balance, but he quickly recovered.

"Trike!" I shouted. "Here, buddy! Quick!"

Trike ran to me. He looked scared and confused, but, other than that, he was unhurt. I swept my arms around him and gave him a big hug. "I'm so glad you're safe, Trike," I said. "You saved my life." Trike licked my face and wagged his tail. I think he was as happy to see me as I was to see him.

"I can't believe that just happened!" Kiera exclaimed as Trike and I raced to the patio. "That thing almost ate your dog!"

"And me, too!" I said.

We stood quietly for a moment, staring at the plant. I wondered if we should call Mom and Dad and tell them what was going on.

No, I thought. They'd never believe me.

Then who? The police? They wouldn't believe me, either.

We were just going to have to stop the monster Venus melon ourselves, and that was all there was to it. I knew that the key to killing the plant was the Whippy Fizz, but I couldn't get close enough. Unless—

"That's it!" I cried suddenly. "I think I know how

we can kill the plant!"

"How?" Kiera asked.

"My water cannon! It shoots a stream of water fifty feet! I can fill it with Whippy Fizz and hose down the plant! That will work!"

I hurried into the house, followed by Kiera and Trike. My water cannon was in my closet; I hadn't used it since last summer. I pulled it out and took it to the kitchen. The normal way to fill it was to dip the barrel into the water and pull up on the handle, drawing water in. But because the Whippy Fizz was in a plastic bottle, I had to pour it into the barrel. Kiera held the cannon while I did the pouring. I spilled a little bit on the floor, but I didn't care. I could clean it up later . . . after we'd taken care of the man-eating Venus melon.

When it was filled, I placed the bottle on the counter and took the water cannon from Kiera.

"This will do it, I'm sure," I said confidently.

"I hope so," Kiera said.

I carried the water cannon to the patio. Kiera followed, but Trike turned and went into the living room, picked up his stuffed hedgehog, and sat by the couch. He'd had enough excitement for one day.

At the back of the yard, the Venus melon was motionless, except for gentle, swaying movements caused by a light breeze. In looking at the plant, no one would have any idea how dangerous it was.

Kiera and I, of course, knew better.

"How close are you going to have to get?" Kiera asked.

"I'm not going to get closer than about twenty feet," I replied. "I want to be close enough to give it a good soaking, but I want to be far enough away so that it can't get me again."

"Be careful," she said.

"You told me that last time," I said.

"And it didn't do any good," Kiera replied.

I stepped off the patio and onto the grass, stopping by the trunk of the huge maple tree. I aimed the water cannon at the monster Venus melon at the back of the yard, confident that my plan would work, as I was sure I'd be able to unload all of the Whippy Fizz and soak the plant.

And that's when the plant did the unthinkable.

It pulled its roots from the ground and used them as legs!

If I hadn't been so surprised and horrified, I

might have been able to fire the water cannon filled with Whippy Fizz. But the shock of seeing the plant come alive like it was had completely freaked me out. The gigantic plant was now unearthed, using its long, tentacle-like roots as legs! Not only that, but it was coming for me . . . fast! Even if I soaked the plant with Whippy Fizz, the plant wouldn't die right away. It would still be able to come after me.

I abandoned my plan and turned to run back to the house—but I tripped and fell. The water cannon flew out of my hands, and I landed on it, hitting the ground and nearly knocking the wind from me. I started to get up . . . but it was too late. The monster Venus melon was already upon me.

I was barely aware of Kiera screaming from the patio. I turned my head and rolled in her direction, and that's probably what saved my life. The very instant that I rolled, the gigantic, hungry mouth chomped down on the ground, at the very spot I had been!

But now I had another problem. Now that I knew the monster Venus melon could move, there was no way I would have time to run to the safety of my house.

The tree.

It was my only hope.

I leapt for the first branch and pulled myself up,

swinging my legs over the limb as I reached higher into the tree. I didn't take the time to look down, as I knew that if I did, it might blow my concentration. Right now, I needed to focus on one thing: climbing high enough to get away from that crazy plant.

Kiera had stopped screaming, and now I could hear Trike barking from inside the house. There was no doubt he knew what was happening, and he was going bananas. But it was a good thing he was inside. If he were out, he'd be running around, trying to attack the plant. Now that the plant could run on its own, Trike wouldn't have a fighting chance.

Beneath me, the Venus melon continued attacking. The head-like thing opened its mouth and snapped at the maple branches, snaking its way up the tree.

Think like a squirrel, I thought. Think like a squirrel. That's what I told myself whenever I climbed a tree. Squirrels are some of the best tree climbers in the world, and whenever I climbed a tree, I tried to imagine that I was a squirrel, effortlessly bounding from branch to branch, sure of every move I made. I don't know if it made me a better tree climber or not, but I'd never fallen from a tree.

"Anthony!" Kiera screeched. "Are you all right?!?!"

"I am right now!" I shouted. "If I can keep away from that thing!"

I continued climbing . . . but now, I had another problem.

The Venus melon was climbing, too!

It never occurred to me that a plant could climb. But, then again, it never occurred to me that a plant could pull its own roots from the ground and give chase!

Well, I thought as I continued to climb higher and higher, a watermelon is a vine, and vines can grow in any direction.

But if the monster Venus melon could climb, that would mean that I would soon be trapped. Once I reached the top of the tree, there was nowhere I could go.

"Kiera!" I shouted. "I need your help!"

"What do you want me to do?!?!" she shouted frantically. I couldn't see her because of the thick branches and leaves of the maple tree, but I knew she was still a safe distance away, on the porch.

"Get the water cannon filled with Whippy Fizz!"

I shouted. "Soak the Venus melon! You've got to stop it before it reaches me!"

Kiera didn't say anything, and I could only hope that she was racing to pick up the water cannon and spray the attacking plant. Still, it might be too late . . . but there were no other options.

Meanwhile, I continued to think like a squirrel, grabbing branch after branch, pulling myself higher and higher into the tree. I didn't look down, but I could hear the hungry Venus melon as it, too, climbed the branches of the old maple.

"Kiera!" I shouted. "Hurry! Before the plant gets too high in the tree!"

"I've got it!" Kiera shouted. "But I can't see the plant! It's already hidden by the branches of the other tree!"

That wasn't good news. That meant that my time had just about run out, as I was nearing the top of the tree.

Think like a squirrel. Think like a squirrel.

One advantage I did have was that I'm not very big. Certainly nowhere near the size of the monster Venus melon. There might be a chance I could climb out onto a branch and make my way back down the

tree. Maybe the Venus melon would be too big and heavy, and the maple branches wouldn't be able to support its weight.

As I reached the top of the tree, I looked around for what looked like the strongest branch, one that could support my weight. Finding one, I began climbing out onto it.

Think like a squirrel. Think like a squirrel.

As I made my way cautiously onto the branch, it began to bend. Below me, I could hear the Venus melon continuing to climb, and I knew that if my plan didn't work, my time was up. The branch continued to bend until it touched another limb. I let go of the branch I was holding and grasped the one directly below me, wrapping my arms around it and holding on with everything I had. Branches scraped my face and arms, but I hardly felt them. Scratches were nothing compared to what the monster Venus melon could do to me.

I dropped down to the next branch. Now, the enormous plant and I were at the same level in the tree. It, however, was near the trunk, and I was on the very outer edge of the branches.

It's working! I thought. It's too heavy, and it

knows it can't come out this far because the branches wouldn't be able to support its weight!

That was the last thing I thought when I heard a sudden, loud snap! The branch I had been on gave way, and I was falling, falling, on a collision course with the ground, head first.

12

Branches smacked my legs, arms, and head. One hit me directly in the stomach and knocked the wind from my lungs. None of them, however, broke my fall. The only thing they did was knock me around as I continued to plummet toward the ground. I tried to grab one of them, tried to hold on, to stop myself from falling, but I failed. I was moving too fast, and everything around me was a tornado-like blur of branches, stems, and leaves.

In a way, I had succeeded in doing what I wanted to do: get away from the monster Venus melon. But falling to the ground from thirty feet in the

air wasn't what I'd planned. I had been hopeful I would make it, but I hadn't been so lucky.

One last branch hit my shoulder and flipped me over. I was looking up into the tree, in a free fall. In one second, I would hit the ground, and it would be all over. The last thing I heard was Kiera scream. Then, everything went black.

"Ow!" Kiera wailed. "That hurt! You just about killed me!"

I opened my eyes.

The branches of the maple tree flared out above me. During my fall, I'd knocked a few leaves loose, and they tumbled and fluttered down like fat, green hands. A few scattered rays of sunlight streamed through.

"Get off me!" Kiera yelped, and in a strange realization, I suddenly figured out that I wasn't dead. Kiera was beneath me. I had landed on top of her, and she had broken my fall.

I rolled to the side. My arm hurt, and there was a small cut on my hand. Nothing serious.

Kiera was sprawled out in the grass, and she got to her knees.

"You landed right on top of me!" she said.

"You saved my life," I said.

"It was only by accident," Kiera said, brushing away blades of grass from her shirt and pants. "But I'm glad it happened, I guess."

"Are you okay?" I asked.

"Yeah," Kiera replied, rubbing her head. "But you sure hit me hard."

"I didn't mean to," I said. "But if you hadn't been where you were, I would be dead by now."

It suddenly occurred to me that my life had been saved twice that day: once by Trike, the other by Kiera. I sure was lucky to have such good friends. I know that Kiera hadn't intended to save my life, but she had been in the right place at the right time, and I sure was thankful.

Unfortunately, the fall had broken my water cannon. It lay on the grass in two pieces. The Whippy Fizz had spilled out and soaked into the ground.

And in the tree, the monster Venus melon was descending.

"That thing isn't going to give up," Kiera said.

"And neither can we," I said. "We have to stop it. After all: we created it. What if that thing gets any bigger? He could take over the whole neighborhood. There are people and pets everywhere. Sooner or later,

someone is going to get hurt . . . or worse."

"But Anthony," Kiera pleaded. "We can't keep on trying to take on that thing by ourselves. It's too big and dangerous."

"All we have to do is soak that thing with Whippy Fizz," I replied.

"But the water cannon is broken," Kiera said. She sounded defeated, without hope, desperate.

In the tree, we could see branches moving and swaying as the monster Venus melon made its way back down the tree.

"Well, we'd better think of something, and fast," I said. "That thing is going to—"

Suddenly, in the maple above, the huge Venus melon came into view, but it was no longer climbing. It was dropping through the branches, coming down right on top of us!

"Run!" I shouted as the plant creature came down. It landed upright, on its roots, like a leafy, green gymnast. Trouble was, it came down between us and the house, blocking our way. I'd hoped we would be able to get inside our home and lock the doors. Fat chance of that now.

Kiera took off in one direction, and I took off in

the other. Without a moment's hesitation, the man-eating plant took off after Kiera. It was much faster than she was, and Kiera was quickly knocked to the ground by one of its branches.

Then: the absolute worst happened. The mouth came down upon her and tried to scoop her up. Kiera was kicking and screaming so hard that the plant didn't succeed; however, it was able to grab her entire left leg in its mouth and pull her into the air, leaving her dangling helplessly, kicking and screaming.

I had to act fast, but what could I do? There was no time to go inside to get the Whippy Fizz. And I alone was certainly no match for the thing.

I looked around the yard for anything I could use to fight off the plant. A birdbath? No. Lawn chair? Nope.

And then I saw something that gave me hope.

The garden hose.

There was a spray nozzle attached to it; Mom used it to water her flower garden. I doubted that the stiff stream of water would hurt the plant, but it might distract it enough to drop Kiera so she could get away.

I ran to the spigot and turned the water on. Then, I raced back and picked up the garden hose,

aiming the nozzle like a gun. I grasped the handle and water shot out in a rapid, thick stream.

Meanwhile, Kiera was still in the jaws of the monster Venus melon, swinging upside down, kicking and screaming. I raced toward the plant and began shooting the steady stream of water at it.

The tactic worked. The plant dropped Kiera, and she landed sideways on the ground, where she quickly leapt to her feet and began running toward the house, still shrieking her head off. The plant, meanwhile, was gulping down the water I was spraying at it.

But now I had a chance. I dropped the hose, turned, and sprinted after Kiera. We both made it to the back door at the same time and flew inside. I slammed the door shut.

"We made it!" Kiera gasped. "We're safe!"

"Not necessarily," I said. "That thing still might try to get at us. I'm sure it's strong enough to break through the windows."

"But we're a lot better off in here than we were out there," Kiera said.

We looked out the window at the plant, which wasn't moving. It was just standing there, on its roots,

frozen. Water dripped from its leaves and stems. In the sunlight, the plant looked shiny and bright.

"Maybe the water did something to it," said Kiera.

"Maybe," I said.

Well, the water did something to it, all right. And a really, really bad day was about to get a lot worse.

13

The plant began to grow, right before our eyes.

I should have known it would happen. After all: the plant had nearly tripled in size the day after the thunderstorm. Now, with fresh water to drink, the monster Venus melon was growing again. We could actually see the stems and leaves reaching for the sky, basking in the sunlight.

"It's growing!" Kiera said. She sounded panicky. "It's growing bigger and bigger!"

Still, we were inside the house, and I felt a lot safer here than outside.

"I'll call Dad at work," I said, racing to the

phone. "He'll know what to do."

"He's not going to believe you," Kiera said.

"He has to," I said. "This is an emergency." I picked up the phone and quickly punched in my dad's phone number at work. He answered on the second ring.

"Dad!" I said. "You've got to come home quick. Our plant—the Venus melon—is out of control. It's taller than the house, and it's attacking us!"

There was a pause, then Dad spoke. "Anthony," he said, "this might be your idea of a joke, but I'm at work. I'm very busy."

"Dad, this is no joke. I wouldn't call you unless I was serious. We sprayed water on the plant, and now it's growing even bigger. The thing is really dangerous, Dad. It might take over the neighborhood!"

"That's enough," Dad said. Anger was beginning to boil in his voice. "Now, if you had a real emergency, I'd be happy to help. But I don't have time for jokes. I'll see you tonight." There was a click on the other end of the line. Dad had hung up.

"I'm not giving up," I said. "I'm going to dial 9-1-1." I poked the numbers on the telephone keypad, and the call was answered instantly.

"My name is Anthony Paslaski," I said, "and I have an emergency."

"Go ahead," a very serious-sounding woman said.

"There's a giant plant in our backyard, and it's getting huge. It's already attacked me and my friend and my dog. If it gets much bigger, there might not be any way to stop it."

Kiera spoke. "Tell them we need the police," she said.

"We need the police," I repeated into the phone.

"And the Air Force," Kiera said.

"And the Air Force," I told the woman on the phone.

"Young man," the woman said sternly, "you may not know this, but it is against the law to call this number to play pranks."

"But it's not a prank!" I insisted. "It's our science experiment that's gone bad! We're in serious trouble, and we need the police!"

"And the Air Force," said Kiera.

"And the Air Force," I repeated.

"Oh, I have half a mind to send the police to your home," the woman said angrily. "Now, I'm going

to hang up, and if you call again, I will send the police, and they will arrest you!"

"Fine!" I said. "Send the police! When they get here, they'll see—"

There was a loud click on the phone. The woman had hung up. Like my dad, she thought I was playing a joke.

"She didn't believe me, either," I said to Kiera. "No one will. It's just too crazy for anyone to believe."

"Except you, me, and Trike," Kiera said.

In the backyard, we could only watch as the monster Venus melon continued to grow. After a while, it stopped. Now, it was nearly half the size of the maple tree. It stood still and motionless, on its roots, looking very innocent.

We, however, knew different. That plant was a killer. It was a bloodthirsty, man-eating carnivore, and now I wondered if we'd ever be able to stop it.

"I'm sure glad we're in here and it's out there," Kiera said.

Then, we had something else to worry about.

A blue ball sailed through the air and bounced into our yard. It rolled to a stop in the grass, only a few feet from the monster Venus melon. Out of the corner

of my eye, I saw another movement.

A boy.

He had been playing by himself in the yard next door, totally unaware of what had been going on. Now, a wild toss had once again landed his ball in our backyard . . . and he had slipped through the bushes and into our yard to retrieve it.

He wasn't going to have a chance.

14

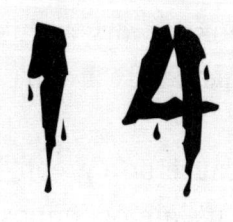

I opened the back door. "Hey!" I yelled.

The boy stopped and looked at me.

"Don't come any closer," I said. "There is a, um, there is a . . ." I was trying to think of something I could tell him, some reason why he should not come into our yard.

"What?" the boy asked. "I just want to get my ball."

"Yes, but there is a dangerous snake out there. Yeah, that's right. We just saw him. He has sharp fangs and is very scary."

The boy looked terrified as his eyes scanned our

backyard. He took a slow step backward, as if the snake might be at his feet.

"Really?" he asked.

"That's right," Kiera said. "You'd better not come any closer. That snake might get you."

The boy looked wary as his eyes searched the grass. He shook his head. "I don't see any snake," he said.

"That's because he's green," I said. "He blends in with the grass. It's almost impossible to see him."

The boy continued to search the grass. He scratched his head. "I don't see any snake," he said.

"Well, he's out there somewhere," I said. "You go home, and when the snake goes away, I'll bring your ball back to you."

For a moment, I thought everything was going to be all right. I thought I had tricked him into believing there was a dangerous snake nearby, and he would return to his own yard.

But the boy must have really wanted his ball, because he suddenly sprang and began running across our lawn, toward his ball. He probably figured that if he ran fast, the snake wouldn't get him. Of course, there wasn't any snake for him to be worried about.

But there was a plant, and that was much worse.

The boy raced toward his ball, and I leapt into action, flying out the back door, bounding over the patio, and into the backyard. He saw me coming and shot me a horrified glance, but he kept running until he reached his ball. Then, he picked it up and turned in one quick motion . . . and that's when the monster Venus melon attacked. It surged forward, and, using its limbs, reached out and grabbed the boy. Horrified, the little kid started screaming like a tea kettle. He twisted and squirmed and wiggled madly, and that's what saved him. He succeeded in freeing himself from the clutches of the plant, and, even more amazing, never let go of his ball. As soon as he was free, he ran across the grass, through the bushes, and he never looked back. I was sure he was going to have nightmares for weeks.

And now I had another problem: me. The plant had spotted me in the yard and was already making a mad dash in my direction. Again, I was amazed—and horrified—at how fast the thing could move, running on its roots.

"Anthony!" Kiera squealed. "Get back in here!"

I turned and ran toward my house, bounding across the patio and leaping over a lawn chair. Kiera held the door open for me, and I dove inside . . . just as the monster Venus melon lunged. Kiera slammed the door closed just in time, and the huge plant slammed into it, shaking the entire house.

"That was too close," I said, grabbing Kiera by the hand and pulling her away from the door. We backed into the kitchen, wondering what the plant's next move would be. Thankfully, it turned away from the house and went into the yard.

"What if that thing tries to get inside?" Kiera asked.

I shook my head. "We're going to get rid of that thing once and for all," I replied. "I have an idea I should have thought about a long time ago. But it's going to take both of us to do it."

"What's that?" Kiera asked.

"Let's take what's left of the Whippy Fizz," I said, "the entire bottle, and feed it to the plant. We'll leave the lid off, so the pop will drain out. Maybe that will do the trick."

"You mean, like, poison it?" Kiera asked.

I nodded. "Exactly," I replied.

"How are we going to get the bottle into its mouth?"

"We're going to have to trick the thing," I said. "We're going to have to make it eat the bottle. We'll throw the bottle at the plant, and it will gobble it up."

"You're crazy!" Kiera said. "How are you going to get close enough without the plant gobbling you up?!?!"

In the yard, the monster Venus melon stopped. Once again, it was motionless, just like all the other plants, trees, flowers, and shrubs. It looked as harmless as ever.

"Well," I said, "we know that if we go outside, the plant will come after us. But maybe if I throw that bottle of Whippy Fizz at it, that will distract it. It'll grab the bottle out of the air."

"I don't know," Kiera said, shaking her head. "It sounds dangerous."

"Of course it's dangerous," I said. "But we don't have any other choice. We tried calling for help, and no one believes us. If we don't stop that thing ourselves, nobody will. And just think of what will happen if it gets any bigger. It's already taller than our house. Next thing you know, it might be eating cars

and trucks."

I walked to the refrigerator, opened the door, and pulled out the two-liter plastic bottle of Whippy Fizz. The bottle was just over half full, and I hoped it would be enough to do the trick.

"Here's what we'll do," I said. "I'll go into the backyard with the bottle. You stay by the back door and hold it open. I'll chuck the bottle at the plant, then come back. Hopefully, the Venus melon will grab the bottle out of the air."

"But what if it doesn't work?" Kiera asked. "What if the plant attacks you, instead?"

"Let's try not to think about that," I said. "Come on, before that kid comes back into our yard or before that plant starts terrorizing the entire neighborhood."

I walked to the door, carrying the bottle of Whippy Fizz. I unscrewed the cap and placed it on the counter. Outside, the plant remained motionless.

I slowly pushed the door open.

"Remember," I whispered. "Hold the door open. I'll be right back."

Kiera said nothing.

I stepped onto the patio, eyeing the monster Venus melon, trying to estimate how close I would

have to get before I threw the bottle of Whippy Fizz.

I walked across the patio and stepped onto the grass. Behind me, Kiera was standing in the open doorway, holding the back door open.

Step by step, I walked closer and closer to the towering plant. So far, so good. Just a little bit farther . . . .

When I was finally close enough, I drew back my right arm and let the bottle fly. It soared up into the air like a lopsided football, arcing toward the plant, falling down, down—

Suddenly, the giant bulb came to life, rocketing up, its hungry jaws open wide. In one quick motion, its mouth closed down on the bottle of Whippy Fizz.

I didn't wait to see what happened after that. I needed to get back to the house, and fast. I turned and started to run.

Kiera screamed and pointed, just as I was knocked to the ground. I landed flat on my chest, surrounded by stems and leaves. They wrapped around my body, gripping my arms, legs, hands, and neck. It was hard to breathe.

Everything began to go black, and I realized that my plan had failed. The Whippy Fizz hadn't

worked. I was going to be nothing more than plant food.

15

I was suffocating.

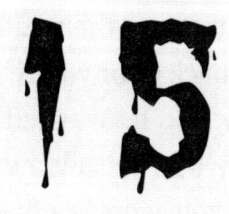

The plant had wrapped its stems and leaves around my entire body, including my neck, cutting off my air. I couldn't breathe, I couldn't speak or scream, and I couldn't move.

In the distance, I could hear Kiera screaming. She was shouting my name, over and over. But there was nothing she could do. She was powerless; I was helpless. Trike was in the house, barking. There was nothing he could do, either.

The plant suddenly stopped moving, and the stem around my neck loosened. I could breathe again, and I drew in a deep, long breath, gasping for more.

The leaves and stems around my body seemed to lose their grip, and I struggled to break free, pulling at the grass, crawling away. The stems and leaves that surrounded me fell away.

Finally, I was free. I wasted no time, bouncing to my feet and running to the patio. I didn't stop until I was through the back door where Kiera waited. Trike was in the kitchen, and he wagged his tail and barked a couple of times when he saw me.

"I thought you were a goner!" Kiera shouted. "That thing trampled you like it was an elephant!"

"That's what it felt like," I said, still gasping for air. "An elephant with tentacles that tried to strangle me."

In the backyard, the plant lay splayed out like a felled tree.

Then, it began to move.

A branch trembled.

A leaf curled and uncurled.

Stems and roots began to writhe like snakes, and the plant began to rise. Soon, it was upright again, standing tall in the sunlight.

"The Whippy Fizz didn't do anything," Kiera said in despair. "The plant is just too powerful."

Kiera was right. There was no way we could stop the plant. What was worse, we couldn't even call for help, because no one believed us. Oh, soon enough, they would. Soon enough, someone else would see the plant, or the plant would begin attacking innocent people. When that happened, of course, people would believe. They would be scared, and for very good reason. They would wonder where such a vicious, bloodthirsty, killer plant came from.

And we'd have to tell them.

We are in a lot of trouble, I thought. I'm going to be grounded until I'm Grandpa's age.

Then, the monster Venus melon began to shake all over, from its roots, through the leaves and branches, right up to the very top. We could even hear the leaves and stems whispering as they trembled, like some mysterious wind was swirling all around it, leaving all other trees and bushes and plants untouched.

"What's happening to it?" Kiera asked.

All of a sudden, the monster Venus melon blew up! Pieces of leafy green vegetation flew out in every direction, flying in the air and coming down on the grass, the patio, the roof of our house—everywhere. A

few tiny green pieces hit me in the chest.

In two seconds, it was all over. The giant monster Venus melon had been reduced to thousands of hunks of green blobs, scattered all over the place.

"I guess the Whippy Fizz worked, after all," I said quietly.

For the next minute, Kiera and I just stared at the green pieces of what had been our science project. I was a little sad that our experiment had come to an end, because that meant that we no longer had a chance of winning at the science fair—which meant no scholarship for Kiera and me to share. On the other hand, we'd probably saved our neighborhood—and the city—from a lot of destruction.

"We should probably clean this mess up before my mom and dad get home," I said. "Wanna help?"

"Sure," Kiera said with a shrug.

We strode outside. Trike followed, warily sniffing the pieces of green, leafy vegetation that had once been our Venus melon. We walked to the garage, and a group of little kids gathered at the edge of the yard, including the one who owned the plastic ball. "We want to see the giant snake," he said. "The one that attacked me."

I shook my head. "He's gone," I said. "There's nothing to worry about. Go back to playing."

"What was that loud noise?" one of the kids asked.

"And what's all this green stuff all over the place?" quizzed another.

"Oh, just plant stuff," I replied. Then, I had an idea. "Hey . . . how would you kids like to earn some money?"

The group became a chattering mob of excitement.

"Okay," I said, "here's what we need. All of these green pieces scattered around the yard need to be picked up. Take them across the street and dump them in the woods. I'll pay each of you twenty-five cents."

The kids began running around like chipmunks, picking up the pieces of what once had been our monster Venus melon. For an hour, they scurried from our yard to the woods like busy bees coming to and from their hive. Kiera and I didn't even have to work! We just watched them do the job themselves. When they were done, I gave each kid a quarter, just like I'd promised. They were as happy as could be.

"All's well that ends well," Kiera said as we watched our young workers walk away.

"Yeah," I said. "We were lucky. Nobody got hurt, and that's what's important."

"And we can still try for the scholarship," Kiera said. "We'll just have to pick a different project."

"Let's pick something a little easier and less dangerous," I said.

Later that evening, during dinner, I told Mom and Dad exactly what had happened that day, right down to every single detail. They just smiled and shook their heads. I knew they wouldn't believe me. Truth, as the saying goes, is often stranger than fiction, and I went to bed thinking that I would never ever have a day as crazy as this one had been.

And that would have been the end of this story, except for one final, horrifying thing that happened the very next day.

I had just finished breakfast, when there was a knock at the front door. It was Kiera, and her face was as white as a ghost.

"What's the matter?" I asked.

"Follow me," was all she said.

I did as she asked, following her as she walked

across the street. When she got to the woods, she stopped.

"What?" I asked. "What's wrong?"

She pointed into the woods. "What do you see?" she asked.

At first, I didn't see anything. But I continued looking, and as I realized what I was seeing, a cold wave of horror nearly swept me off my feet.

Venus melons.

They were growing in the woods, where the kids had dumped the pieces of the plant the day before. The pieces of the plant had taken root overnight, giving birth to dozens and dozens of offspring. Some of the plants were nearly four feet tall. They were everywhere, growing among the trees and brush. I could see their large, round bulbs, some the size of bowling balls. Some looked like they already had begun to form mouths.

"Kiera," I said in a voice just above a whisper, "get all of your allowance money together. We're going to need a lot of Whippy Fizz."

THE END

Johnathan Rand travels internationally for school visits and book signings! For booking information, call:

1 (231) 238-0338!

www.americanchillers.com

NOW . . . FLIP THIS BOOK
OVER TO READ
'ATTACK OF THE
MONSTER VENUS MELON!'

IT'S AN
AMERICAN CHILLERS
DOUBLE THRILLER!

NOW . . . FLIP THIS BOOK
OVER TO READ
'VAMPIRE NATION.'

IT'S AN
AMERICAN CHILLERS
DOUBLE THRILLER